The Lord Who Sneered and Other Tales

By the same author:

Miss Delacourt Speaks Her Mind
Miss Delacourt Has Her Day
Lady Crenshaw's Christmas: A Novella
A Timeless Romance Anthology: Winter
Collection: It Happened Twelfth Night

Lord Haversham Takes Command

The Lord Who Sneered and Other Tales

A Regency Holiday Anthology

Heidi Ashworth

Cover design by Laura J Miller
www.anauthorsart.com

ISBN-13: 978-0615888934
ISBN-10: 0615888933

A Ghost in the Graveyard

England, October 1816

Chapter One

"I trust that should you require anything during your stay," the Dowager Duchess of Marcross said with a ferocious frown, "that you shall be forthcoming. Nothing is more unsatisfactory than to discover one has deprived ones guests of the comforts of life."

Anne Crenshaw, settled by a cheerful fire with a steaming cup of tea, blinked back tears of gratitude. She had not expected the fearsome Dowager to be quite so accommodating a hostess.

"There was hardly the need for them to abandon me," the Dowager continued as if for her ears alone. "They had only to speak up. All should have been arranged to their satisfaction. I suppose you would have preferred to have stayed with them, eh?" demanded Anne's grandmama by marriage.

Perfectly aware that the Dowager referred to her grandson and his wife, Anne felt her eyes go wide as she inwardly bemoaned her timid nature. "Naturally, I have visited Sir Anthony and Lady Crenshaw at Prospero Park," she said around the lump of misgiving in her throat, "and all was as lovely as one might wish. However, I could hardly expect them to take me when they have a new little one of their own and the same age as the Duke's. The Duchess made it very clear that I was much too much in the way. It would be foolish of me to assume Ginny should feel otherwise."

The Dowager gave Anne a hard stare, prompting Anne to wonder if her speech were perhaps a bit too bold. Still, she owned that the company of the infamous virago seated before her was preferable to one moment in the presence of her disdainful father-in-law or his chilly, new duchess.

"Very sensible, Roxanne," the Dowager intoned. "Very sensible, indeed. I should not wish anything to disturb their tranquility after their unseemly haste in acquiring it."

"No, of course not," Anne said in a voice faint with lack of conviction. It would hardly do to shore up Grandmama's antagonistic views with regard to her only living grandson, whose sudden desertion nine months prior in favor of his own establishment, had not been well received. However, any conviction Anne might have possessed when she married Sir Anthony's cousin, Reed, had been drained from her under her father-in-law's thunderous reign. It had seemed pointless to express any opinion he did not share. As such, she had become unaccustomed to speaking up. Nevertheless, the time for forming her own views had finally arrived now that she was no longer under his roof.

"Grandmama, I wonder if you would see fit to call me Anne? It was how I was called by my parents when a child, though I daresay you had not known that."

"No, I had not," Grandmama snapped. "I suppose one might lay the fault for that in my son's dish."

"Well, yes, if I am honest. He feels pet names to be foolish. As it hardly mattered to Reed what I was called, he went along with it. That is not to say he did not care for me," Anne hastened to add. "He was a good man and a good husband, but he has been gone over a year and I feel the need for a new beginning."

"And rightly so!" the Dowager exclaimed with a flourish of her finger. "A new home, a new name and hopefully, before many months have passed, a new husband. No, you mustn't deny me one of my few joys in life," she insisted when taking in what Anne could only assume to be her face turned pale with shock.

"Matchmaking is second nature to me. I am sure to find you a most suitable husband, given enough time. You are still young and, I might add, quite handsome so you may rely on my success in this. However, you must swear that you will put off your blacks immediately. Your widow's weeds are a perfect foil for that abundance of pale hair you have, however, a deep blue or even a red should prove more becoming."

"I believe it is early days, yet, for red," Anne insisted as it dawned on her that the Dowager might actually wish to have her granddaughter-in-law underfoot. Nevertheless, Anne was persuaded little more than a year of widowhood to be insufficiently long to embark on a bid for remarriage. Fortunately, she was saved from stating her opinion on the subject when a maid entered the library with a silver salver bearing a gilt-edged card.

"Oh, no, it's that barmy Lady Avery!" the Dowager cried as she surveyed the card through her lorgnette. "I would deny her, but there is no turning her away once she is set on a piece of nonsense. Show her in, Mary," the Dowager directed with a wave of her hand, "but I must insist you do not bring in a tea tray or she shall never leave us!"

Before the maid had time to so much as bob a curtsy, Lady Avery, her face alight with news of what appeared to be of the most delightful nature, burst into the room. "Eustace's cousin has come to call!" she exclaimed as if this were an announcement of significant import to her stunned listeners. "My dearest husband is so often gone on crucial business that I do believe he felt a guest would serve as a remedy to my *ennui*," she rushed to reveal. "However, I must confess baby Herbert is very absorbing, and all the company I need. So I am afraid he must stay here."

"He, whom?" the Dowager queried. "Surely you do not refer to your infant?"

"*Mais non!*" Lady Avery said with a clap of her hands as she sank into the chair next to Anne, the proximity of which allowed her to discern the fatigue behind Lady Avery's thin smile. "None but I shall ever have her hands on him. Eustace is allowed to hold him when I am not, but that is all."

Anne had been exposed to the Countess of Avery in times past but had never before had quite such an intimate view of the lady's odd behavior nor the opportunity to converse with her. "Lady Avery, how good you are to spend so much time with your baby," she said as she pushed away the pain she felt at her own childlessness. Have you no nursemaid?"

"Who are *you*?" Lady Avery asked with a frosty glare down her nose at Anne. "And, yes, I have a nursemaid, to whom I am very generous as she has naught to do but heat the baby's bottle," she said smugly, "and get up with him during the night and wash his nappies," she added, counting tasks on her fingers. "And clean his clothes, sit by his cot until he falls asleep and hold him when he is sick or fretful during the day, but that is not so very much, is it?" she asked, looking to both Anne and the Dowager for approval.

"Lady Avery," the Dowager Duchess interjected before the young mother had a chance to further elaborate, "what of this cousin of Lord Avery's? And what has he or she to do with us?"

"Oh, but of course! He is quite a favorite of Eustace's; however, he is ancient which I find makes him dreadfully dull. It is small wonder the baby fusses whenever he is about. Surely you must see I can't hold my little Herbert on my lap if he is fussing!"

"No, of course not," Anne said in a pleasant manner designed to distract their guest from the Dowager's fulminating glare.

"I still do not see what this has to do with me, Lady Avery!" the Dowager boomed. "As you might have observed, I am in the midst of entertaining my own houseguest whom I should very much like to make comfortable."

"But that is why it is all so perfect!" Lady Avery said with another clap of her hands. "Willy is without a place to stay and, here you are, practically running a boarding house." Suddenly, she jumped to her feet and ran to the door as she called over her shoulder: "I shall fetch him here this instant!"

Anne had heard much about Lady Avery but nothing she had been told prepared her for what she had just witnessed. "Does she intend to return, do you think?"

"Oh, yes," Grandmama said with a groan. "And with this Willy she tells of in her wake. What kind of man calls himself Willy?" she asked, rolling her eyes heavenward. "And what are we to do with him?"

"What *can* be done?" Anne asked. "It sounds as if Lady Avery has given him little choice in the matter."

"If he is half the self-absorbed toad that his cousin is I shall have him removed forthwith."

Anne felt the Dowager's judgment of Lord Avery to be a bit harsh but knew it unwise to say so. "I have met Lady Avery's husband but infrequently. Is he as distressing as all that?"

"Distressing is not the word I should use," the Dowager said with a heavy sigh as she drew herself into a fully regal position. "But never your fear, I shall be shed of this Willy as soon as I am able."

The Dowager's anger was palpable; Anne dared not so much as shift in her chair, so oppressive was the atmosphere in the room. The moments of silence that followed were punctuated only by the ticking of the mantle clock and the occasional ember popping in the fire.

Finally, a commotion was heard out in the passage and the door thrown open. "Here is our Willy!" Lady Avery cried as she once again burst into the room, dragging a man, as tall as he was hesitant, behind her. "He is a bit bashful, but I am persuaded you shall have much to talk about," she babbled as she led her reluctant relation to the fire and pushed him into the chair closest to Anne. "Well, then," she said as if ridding herself of a great burden, "I am off to sing to my sweet little Herbert." Without so much as a word of farewell, she was gone.

There was a moment of dismayed silence during which Grandmama's latest guest stared at the tips of his shoes and the Dowager looked everywhere but at him. It afforded Anne the opportunity to study his profile in the late-afternoon light, though little information was to be gained from the view of his profile except that he was possessed of a head of tidy, light brown curls swept forward along a high brow and a long face that easily accommodated a somewhat prominent nose and chin. It was impossible to evaluate his eyes as fine or otherwise in such low light, and Anne realized it was up to her to set matters to rights.

"Shall I ring for a tray, Grandmama?" she asked, her low voice cutting into the silence. As there was no reply Anne was left with nothing to do but rise and pull the bell, whereupon she searched for the tinder and flint to light the various candles throughout the room. "There, that is much better," she mused and turned to find herself under scrutiny by Lord Avery's cousin.

It seemed he was surprised to be caught out gazing at her as he immediately dropped his gaze and returned to the contemplation of his shoes.

Anne stole a glance at Grandmama, who sat with her chin settled in the cleft of her abundant bosom amidst the faint rumbling of her snores. "Oh, dear, it would seem she has fallen asleep. I suppose introductions have been left to me. I am Mrs. Crenshaw," she explained as she returned to her seat by the fire, "but there is no need to stand on ceremony with me. I would very much prefer to be called Anne." As this speech produced no reply, she leaned forward to better look into his face. "I'm afraid we have been given little to go on. We don't even know what we should call you."

"You should call me humiliated," he replied in a voice so deep as to be positively startling. "I pray you to consider," he added, lifting his gaze from his shoes and returning her look with a frank one of his own, "I hadn't any idea as to Lady Avery's intention and am, I can only speculate, abandoned here with no baggage or possession whatsoever, and no conveyance to hasten my departure. I haven't even a proper black suit should I not be put out on the stoop before it is time to change for dinner."

"Oh," Anne said as surprised by his words as the wealth of good humor evident in his large eyes, so brown as to be nearly black and free of any sign of age. Lady Avery could only have been exaggerating when she used the word 'ancient' to describe her cousin. Privately, Anne thought the evening suit to be no sad loss; his day suit of dove gray set off to perfection by a paler gray waistcoat and pantaloons was the most beautiful she had seen and fit his trim form like a glove. "I am persuaded Grandmama will understand. I have been displaced by virtue of a new arrival, as well, and she has been nothing but generosity itself. Should you stay there is room enough, and I, for one, should be glad of the company."

The stranger sat up straighter in his chair and seemed to take in his surroundings for the first time. "Am I misinformed when told this is the house of the Dowager Duchess of Marcross?"

"You are not, and this," Anne said with a nod that indicated Grandmama, "is the Dowager Duchess, herself. However, I must protest; you have not as yet introduced yourself. I believe the Countess referred to you as Willy. Shall we so do, as well?"

"My cousin's wife is certainly a force with which to be reckoned," he said with a self-conscious adjustment to his crisp, white cravat. "My parents, Mr. and Mrs. Williams, christened me Theodore, but my mother has called me Theo since I was in short coats." With that revelation, he seemed to relax and turned to favor her with a small smile.

"Which begs the question, why 'Willy' when you might have been called 'Teddy' any day of the week?" Anne quizzed.

"I'm afraid the responsibility for that must be laid at the door of family tradition," he replied with a more natural smile that lit his entire face.

"I see," Anne replied, more than a little dazzled by the sweetness of his expression. "Do tell of your family. I am aware that you are Lord Avery's cousin, though not a Haversham."

"My beloved mother is the half sister of my cousin, the Earl. As for myself, I possess no title with which to encumber my name."

"Nor do I. That is, to say, my husband, the Dowager Duchess' grandson, was heir to his father, the Duke. Now the new babe has all the titles my husband once bore, and I am left with little but a place at the table. I suppose one might rightfully refer to me as Lady Crenshaw, but we already have one of those in the neighborhood and I refuse to countenance 'the Dowager Countess' for a single moment."

Mr. Williams cocked his head and looked at her as if for the first time. "You are a widow, then, Mrs. Crenshaw," he remarked, gently.

"Just above a year," she replied, his kindness inducing a fluttering in her heart she thought she should never feel again.

He reached his hand across the table between them almost as if he dared to take her hand, but he seemed to think better of it and pulled it back. "May I offer you my most sincere condolences?"

"Thank you, Mr. Williams." She felt unsure of, and a little breathless, at the direction their conversation was leading. "You are very kind. I think perhaps you are not unacquainted with grief?"

"Not of such a personal nature," he replied, revealing nary a clue as to his own marital status.

Anne took herself to task for so much as wondering if he had a wife tucked away at home even as she noted how far from accurate Lady Avery's description of her cousin had been. Not only was he not in the least ancient, he was, in fact, still a young man, though certainly old enough to have been married for some time. Anne might have pressed him further, but it was at this moment the maid entered the room with the tea cart, prompting Mr. Williams to rise to his feet in order that the cart should be placed between himself and the Dowager Duchess without his knees posing a hazard to the operation.

"I shall just move my chair back a bit," he suggested.

As he did so, Anne observed how the Dowager was awakened by the small commotion in the room. She, however, said not a word. Anne hoped that the Dowager's reticence to speak was not a sign that she should choose to have Mr. Williams removed from the premises. Yet, once they had filled their plates, Anne was pleased that the Dowager remained silent as it allowed her presence to be almost entirely forgotten. As such, Anne and Mr. Williams were afforded the freedom to converse without the Dowager's usual quenching remarks.

Just as Anne was entertaining thoughts of supreme contentment in her tea-time companion, the Dowager stirred, leaving Anne in some anxiety as to just how long her grandmama had been awake.

"I believe, Mr. Williams, that you require an evening suit," the Dowager remarked. "I shall send a footman to the Abbey to fetch yours here before time to dress for dinner."

"That is most kind of you, Your Grace," Mr. Williams replied. "If it does not prove inconvenient, I should like to have the rest of my things retrieved, as well."

Anne held back a gasp at his daring but, to her great astonishment, heard herself add her request to his own. "Yes, Grandmama, I do believe we should very much enjoy Mr. Williams' company for as long as it is tenable. That is to say, should he desire to stay," she added hopefully.

"Very well, then," the Dowager said as she rose to her feet. "I shall have all of your things brought if that is what you wish, Mr. Williams."

"I assure you that it is," Mr. Williams replied as he also rose to his feet and favored the Dowager with an exquisite bow.

Anne, delighted at how well her visit to Dunsmere was proceeding, remained seated in veiled observation of the increasingly attractive Mr. Williams until she was roused from her woolgathering by a deep "harrumph" from the Dowager.

"Roxanne, I do believe you are wanted elsewhere."

"Yes, of course, Grandmama," she said as she rose to her feet. As she followed the Dowager from the room, and up the stairs, she suddenly felt it quite appropriate to put off her widow's weeds and don colors, forthwith. A dark blue for dinner would surely be acceptable and not in the least disrespectful towards the memory of her dead husband. However, she had precious little else but black gowns with her. Confounded at her own audacity at the very idea, Anne drew alongside the Dowager and spoke without having first been addressed.

"Grandmama, I do believe you are most correct with regard to putting off my blacks. I should like to do as you suggest but haven't but one or two gowns other than mourning in my trunks. Might a footman be sent for the rest of my wardrobe, as well?"

"Don't be a fool, Roxanne; those gowns are nearly two years out of fashion. I shall send for my mantua maker and have you measured for a new wardrobe tomorrow morning."

Anne might have argued. Indeed, she should have; the expense would be enormous and she was not the responsibility of her husband's grandmama. Yet, however much she wished to resist, she knew it pointless to try. Instead, she allowed herself a moment of private glee before expressing her gratitude to the Dowager for her tremendous generosity.

"There is no need to thank me, Roxanne. Did I not say that it was time to forge a new life for yourself?"

"Yes, Grandmama, you did, but I had never expected. . ."

"Of course you had not! Nor had you expected to be a widow at such a young age, I surmise, but here you are. Now!" she continued on despite Anne's attempts to speak, "it is my intention to hold a ball. The one I arranged at Christmas-last served to remind me how very much I enjoy such affairs. You shall have a gown made up expressly for my first ever Harvest Ball, one of periwinkle, I think, to match the unusual shade of your eyes. I am persuaded I have never seen another pair like them. Naturally you shall wear my *parure* of amethysts as they will set off your eyes to perfection!"

"But, you must not, Grandmama. They are much too fine for me."

"Nothing is too fine for any relation of mine. You must remember that, Roxanne," the Dowager said as she paused in front of her chamber door and looked at her grandson's widow for the first time during the course of their conversation. "Yes, I am persuaded I am absolutely correct about the amethysts. It isn't as if I shall ever again have occasion to wear them."

"If you insist, I shall wear them, and gladly," Anne said meekly. "And, I must agree, a ball should be lovely. It shall give me plenty to do in helping with preparations. I only wonder if perhaps the sudden commitment of our resources might not be at the expense of Mr. Williams."

The Dowager looked down her nose at Anne; a preposterous feat at best considering how petite the old lady was in comparison to Anne's more than average height. "As to Mr. Williams, we shall see."

Anne knew this pronouncement to be her dismissal. After bobbing a curtsy, she turned down the passage towards her own room and wondered which chamber the Dowager would give Mr. Williams should she allow him to stay, then blushed at such temerity as to entertain thoughts so inappropriate. With a sigh, she entered her room and laid down on her bed to rest before dinner. However, the novelty of wearing colors again filled her once again with glee, making sleep impossible until, quite without warning, the face of her husband rose into her mind.

Assailed by a wave of guilt, she thought perhaps it *was* wrong to think of giving up her formal mourning quite so soon.

Resolved to speak to the Dowager about it directly after dinner, Anne slipped into slumber and dreamt of a blanket of purple crocus blooming amongst a field of snow.

She woke refreshed and feeling more hopeful than she had in many a year. With fingers that trembled a bit with anticipation, she donned the dark blue dress but regretted that it was still so close to black as to make little difference. It was then she remembered that she had with her the peacock colored shawl given her by her husband shortly before he died and which she had never worn. She hadn't intended on wearing it during her stay at Dunsmere but had been so delighted by its beauty when first she drew it forth from its tissue that she could not bear to leave it behind.

Determined to begin anew, she draped the bright paisley-patterned shawl around her shoulders and opened the door to find a maid with her fist raised as if she were about to knock.

"Oh! Beggin' your pardon, Missus, but Her Grace has sent me to do up your hair."

Anne had rarely bothered to seek help in arranging her long, golden locks; her hair required little artifice or ornamentation and she was able to accomplish simple styles with ease. "That will be lovely, however, if you are needed elsewhere, I am most content to leave it be."

"Your hair is beautiful if you pardon me sayin' so, Missus," the maid said as she entered the room and shut the door behind her. "But, there's nothing I should like better than to make it shine!"

"Well, then," Anne replied as she sat herself at the dressing table, "I shall enjoy watching you." In the end, Anne was absolutely fascinated with the efforts of the maid who divided a simple twisted bun into a convoluted style of curls, braids and tendrils of gold that took Anne's breath away. As she gazed at her reflection in the mirror, she felt as if her new life had well and truly begun.

Chapter Two

After a week as a guest at Dunsmere, Mr. Theodore Williams was beginning to feel a bit like Scheherazade. Each evening, as he had bid the ladies good night, he had been awarded the gift of another twenty-four hour stay by the formidable Dowager Duchess. He would have long ago taken himself off through one means or another if it weren't for the lovely and gracious Mrs. Anne Crenshaw. He had known her to be lovely the moment he first laid eyes on her. He had known her to be gracious after ten minutes spent in her company. However, he hadn't known her to be the most compelling woman he had had the good fortune to meet until she had come down for dinner that first night, her hair like spun gold and her eyes glowing with an inner fire that had somehow before gone unnoticed.

From that moment on, he desired nothing more than to be near her. Whether they were cataloging the roses in order to know better which bushes should be in bloom on the day of the ball, writing out place cards for seating arrangements at supper, or assisting the maids with the polishing of the silver, it was all pure contentment if he were by her side.

It required two whole days before he had enough confidence to suggest they take out the horses for a ride through the park of a morning. After three, he dared to hope Anne might accompany him into the village to shop and visit the circulating library once he had charmed the Dowager into the loan of her carriage and team. It was five days before he felt it appropriate to invite Anne to walk with him through the gardens for a spell after tea, something with which she agreed to with an alacrity that pleased him to no end.

When he considered the minutes and hours they spent together, they seemed to be filled with sunshine and laughter. However, there were long stretches of time during which he had only his thoughts to keep him company. These were sad times, indeed. Especially difficult was the day of the ball as Anne was far too busy to spend even a moment with Theo, a circumstance that felt particularly cruel as he was persuaded it would be his last at Dunsmere.

"I am so sorry, Mr. Williams," she said at breakfast, a meal they took together each day while the Dowager had her roll and hot chocolate in her room. "I am afraid there is no time for a ride today. There is just too much to be done in preparation for tonight."

"I am at your service, as ever, Mrs. Crenshaw. You are already fully aware that I am a dab hand at writing out invitations."

"Yes, of course you are, and it is so very kind of you to wish to help, but all the invitations have been written long since and all that remains is women's work."

"You wound me!" he said with a smile that thoroughly belied his words. "Do you mean to imply that polishing silver and writing place cards is the sole province of men?"

She laughed, a delightful sound that never failed to inspire him to consider how he might inspire more.

"You try my patience, Mr. Williams! You may rest assured that were I to embark on any task today at which you might be useful, I should most certainly request your aid."

"In that case I shall await word from you with bated breath," he said with another smile, this one designed to bend her to his will.

"Now, now, Mr. Williams," she said as she rose to her feet, "I should not if I were you. I am perfectly honest when I say that you have naught to do today but wait until the ball. I assure you it shall be worth your tolerance."

Theo rose to his feet, as well, and allowed himself the indulgence of openly observing her as she turned away and walked from the room. He thought, not for the first time, how very different Anne Crenshaw was from the other women he had met. She did not seem bent on attracting him, though she did exactly that with every word and movement, nor did she did speak ill of others in spite of sharing a roof with a veritable diamond mine of inspiration in the Dowager Duchess. Finally, despite her lowered circumstances following the death of her husband, she bore an aura of good will that could not help but lift all in her orbit.

In point of fact, she seemed the sun to which all others were drawn and circled about in perfect amity. His time in the sun required he wait until the ball, however, so he borrowed a steed from Dunsmere's excellent stables and took himself off for the better part of the day. Upon his return, he was struck by how much he missed the warm welcome Mrs. Crenshaw offered whenever he re-entered the house. Realizing she was a woman of her word, he accepted that he should have no glimpse of her until the ball and spent the remainder of the afternoon in his room.

When the gong rang for dinner, he emerged dressed in his best black formal evening suit and the most natty neck cloth arrangement at his command only to find the dining room deserted and a single place set at table. Though he was quite accustomed to being his butler's sole responsibility at many a meal, the absence of the women of the household proved to feel more solitary than when he dined alone at home. With a sigh, he picked up his fork and made his way through the meal, followed by his removal to the drawing room before there came any sign that he was not, save the servants, the sole occupant of the house.

His wait was well rewarded, however, when Mrs. Crenshaw entered the drawing room, and he was once again warmed in the glow of her shining presence. She had confided in him that she had only recently cast off her mourning, but her bright lavender ball gown was a stunning departure from the subdued, lighter-hued gowns she had been wearing the past week. It was cut to perfection from sumptuous satin, the tiny puffed sleeves and bodice overlaid with white lace of a most intricate pattern and brought together at the high waist by a silver ribbon. She wore another in her hair, which was piled high on her head in a labyrinth of gold, and her feet were adorned with silver dancing slippers.

Most eye-catching, after the glow of her face, was the white curve of her neck, graced by a triple pendant of large amethysts. Their brilliance was echoed in the jeweled pins in her hair, as well as the earrings and the cuff of jewels she wore on her wrist. Nevertheless, once he dared look into her eyes, these were all pale shadows in comparison.

"Mrs. Crenshaw," he breathed even as he prayed his jaw had not, indeed, fallen open upon sight of her. "I am persuaded I have never seen anything or anyone more welcome."

"I thank you, Mr. Williams," she replied demurely, her eyes downcast. "Grandmama has requested that you escort me to the ballroom."

He held out his hand to her, and she looked up long enough to allow him yet another dazzling view of her eyes. "I should be devastated should I not have been allowed to provide such a service," he said as she took his arm and they walked from the room. Having such a creature on his arm, one whose exquisite appearance was eclipsed only by the goodness of her heart, was celestial glory, indeed. As they approached the large, double doors to the ballroom, he felt they were the pearly gates and heaven lay on the other side.

A footman played the role of Peter and pushed open the doors to reveal a room blazing with all the colors of the sun. Enormous arrangements of red and yellow roses paired with sprigs of autumn leaves, as well as clusters of late heliotrope and dry lavender, were placed on tables and pillars all about the room. Baskets of melons and squash in the same hues placed in drifts of orange and yellow leaves brightened the corners of the room where the light of the chandeliers, groaning under the weight of scores of blazing candles, did not quite touch.

On a long table, winking in the glow of the candles, as well as the two massive fireplaces, one at either end of the room, was a row of sterling silver punch bowls, each more elegant than the last, interspersed with platters of punch cups and crystal champagne goblets.

"It would seem the Dowager considers dancing thirsty work," he remarked.

"No, it is I!" she insisted. "That is to say, I expect our guests to feel quite thirsty. I don't intend on dancing enough to require much in the way of punch."

"Why ever not, Mrs. Crenshaw? I am persuaded you shall be asked to dance every set." She most assuredly would if he were free to claim each one.

"Oh, no, I think not. I am so recently out of mourning and my family will be present. I am already in the Duke's black books, and he would not be best pleased to see me enjoying myself overly much."

He bent to better look into her face. "But you enjoy dancing, do you not?"

"Oh, indeed, yes!" she said as her cheeks turned a delightful shade of pink. "That is to say, should I be asked, I would most certainly enjoy dancing a set or two."

"Then let me be the first to claim one. Would it be precipitous of me to ask for the first?" It seemed an eternity before her reply and his heart hammered so in his chest that he felt sure she could hear it as well as he.

"Yes, of course, Mr. Williams, I should be delighted." There was nothing out of the ordinary in her answering smile; the same warm smile she had graced him with every day since his arrival and that, to his great disappointment, offered no indication as to how she felt about giving away her first dance to plain Mr. Williams.

Before long the Dowager entered the room, and the other guests began to arrive. The orchestra struck the music for the first set, a lively contra dance, which did not allow for much conversation. Instead, whenever Theo could drag his attention away from Mrs. Crenshaw's graceful form, he considered her reluctance to dance and how he might contrive a means to stay by her side once the set had commenced. However, they were only a few minutes into the set before his thoughts were checked by a commotion at the entrance to the ballroom.

"I will not remain calm!" came a voice Theo thought he knew only too well. "I am a countess, and I shall be as unruly as I please!" This overly-loud pronouncement was followed by, first, a profound hush, then a mumbled speech from person unknown and, finally, a cacophonous wail from an infant, one who was unaccountably, and without a doubt, present in the room.

"Mr. Williams, I do believe your cousins, Lord and Lady Avery, have arrived," Mrs. Crenshaw pointed out. "I can hardly credit it, but it would seem she has brought along her baby! What shall we do? I fear Grandmama will have an apoplexy."

Theo hadn't an idea as to what was happening, but it was a chance to remain by Mrs. Crenshaw's side, so he took her arm and they followed the sound of Lady Avery's voice.

"I do not throw tantrums over trifles, Sir, I can assure you! I saw a ghost in the graveyard next to the church we passed on our way up the drive, and if I say there was a ghost, you may rest assured there *was* a ghost!" Another shriek from the baby followed, one more resounding, if possible, than the last. Theo took a cup of punch from the table as they passed by and held it out to Lady Avery, whilst Mrs. Crenshaw attempted to take the baby from its mother.

"Lady Avery, you must have had quite a turn. See here, your cousin Willy has some refreshment for you. Might I take your darling baby so that you might have a drink?"

Lady Avery turned to look on them with suspicion but relaxed when she saw the deference in their manners. "Why, yes, you may. His name is Herbert but do not say so aloud; for some reason he cries when he hears it."

"I prefer to call him Harry, myself," Lord Avery said in a voice not meant for his wife's ears. "Isn't he a capital little man?" he asked with the air of a man whose confidence had been bolstered by one too many post-dinner brandies.

"Yes, indeed, he is the very picture!" Mrs. Crenshaw said as she took in the sad, little infant dressed in a miniature evening suit rather than the long batiste gown worn by every other infant in the realm.

Theo handed Lady Avery the cup of punch which she drained almost instantly. "I should like another!"

"I shall acquire one for you, my flower!" Lord Avery said and he lost no time in making his escape.

"So this is little Herbert!" said a lovely woman with dark hair who approached on the arm of the most dashingly dressed man in the room. "Anne, do allow me a turn at holding him if you tire."

Mrs. Crenshaw laughed. "You have enough of holding babies with your own little boy."

"Yes, but I am persuaded he is much happier without such tight-fitting clothing. Poor darling!" the dark-haired lady said as she leaned over to peer into the red face of the infant Anne held in her arms.

"Mr. Williams," Mrs. Crenshaw said, "may I make known Her Grace's grandson, Sir Anthony, and his wife, Lady Crenshaw?"

"Yes, of course," Theo said as he took the lady's hand and bowed over it. "And, Sir Anthony," he added with a shake of his hand. "I have oft' heard the name fall from Her Grace's lips."

Sir Anthony smiled. "I fear my wife and I have proved a sad disappointment to dearest Grandmama. However, I am to understand you and Roxanne are compensating for our absence to admiration."

"You must find the means to keep baby Herbert at Dunsmere," Lady Crenshaw said with a fond look for her husband, "and only then shall Her Grace be satisfied enough to forgive you."

"Well, I shall not forgive you," Lady Avery interjected. "And, I am still waiting, I will have you know, for my second cup of punch."

Without a word, Sir Anthony steered his wife towards the dance floor as Lady Crenshaw looked over her shoulder and raised her eyebrows at Anne in apology as they went.

"Well! I have never been so insulted in all my life!" Lady Avery exclaimed.

"Perhaps I might prove to be of service," Theo said in desperation. "I am persuaded my cousin shall appear with your punch at any moment. Why don't you sit here on this very comfortable sofa," he said as he took her arm and led her to one side of the room. "Here you might bounce your son on your knee," he added as he took the baby from Anne and handed him over to his mother, "while Mrs. Crenshaw and I brave the graveyard in search of your ghost."

"Oh, Willy!" Lady Avery said as she attempted to clap her hands around an armful of baby. "You are brilliant! Do be sure to return before the ball is over so that I may learn what you discover."

Theo turned to look a question at Mrs. Crenshaw and was gratified to see that she looked back at him with the very same expression in her eyes. Biting back a smile, she assured Lady Avery that they would not be long outside.

"Oh, but I am persuaded ghost-hunting is a lengthy endeavor," Lady Avery insisted. "How are you to catch a ghost if you don't lie in wait until midnight?"

"Yes," Theo echoed, "how?" A means of keeping Mrs. Crenshaw tethered to this side for the evening had neatly fallen into his lap, and he was not about to let it lie fallow. "Perhaps you should get a wrap," he suggested with what he suspected was a bit of a devilish smile.

Her eyes grew rather large, and he thought for a moment that she would surely object. Instead, she said: "Very well," in low tones meant for his ears alone. "But you must allow me a few moments before you follow me out."

Hardly believing his good fortune, Theo took his leave of Lady Avery, whose attention was now wholly taken up with her babe, and went in search of his cousin who had lingered at the punch table a bit longer than expected. "Avery," he said as he shook his cousin's hand. "You have a fine son. I hope to have one as fine some day."

"Oh, had you thought of marriage already, Theo?"

"I hadn't, truly, until very recently," Theo said as her brought his own cup of punch to his lips.

"Oh, pish!" Avery said with a flap of his hand. "You have years yet before you need find it necessary to set up your nursery. Take it from me," he added as he placed a finger to the side of his nose and winked. "Marriage is not as entirely blissful as the poets make it out to be."

"Forgive me, cousin, but blissful is not the appellation that comes first to mind when I consider your circumstances," Theo said in hopes that his cousin was too drunk to take offense.

"Eh?" Avery asked, favoring his drink with a cross-eyed stare.

As it was clear that Avery was too drunk, even, for proper conversation, Theo felt free to take his leave and make a circuit or two of the room before he made his way through the double doors and down the stairs to the ground floor where he waited for Mrs. Crenshaw to appear. He had not long to wait before he spotted her at the top of the stairs, a thick cloak over one arm. Perhaps she was as anxious to spend time together as was he. The thought warmed him so that he hardly felt the cold air as they quit the house and started down the walkway towards the chapel.

The air was not only chill, but damp, and tendrils of mist wafted across the moon in concourse with the cries of hoot owls and the rustle of dry leaves scurrying across the path at their feet. It seemed the ideal atmosphere to spot a spook if indeed one existed, a circumstance Theo rather doubted. It seemed a good excuse, though, to take Mrs. Crenshaw's arm; she leaned into him with such responsiveness he wondered if she might be afraid. Indeed, the mood was such that he thought it would be necessary for him to cast about for an appropriate topic of conversation and was relieved to find that Mrs. Crenshaw seemed full of questions.

"We have spoken of so much this past week, Mr. Williams, yet I still do not know from where you come. Are you a London bachelor or do you spend some time in the country, as well?"

"I stay in London when I have business in town, but I spend most of my time in the house in which I grew up. It's in a tiny village near Shrewsbury in Shropshire." He wondered if the country appealed to her as much as he hoped or if perhaps he should have first mentioned the stately Georgian townhouse he owned in Holborn in the case she preferred city life.

"Shrewsbury! I am persuaded there is not a lovelier spot on earth," she said, squeezing his arm. "My dear Aunt Simpkins and her husband live very near. I have spent many a happy hour in the vicinity."

Theo felt a spontaneous smile curve his lips and blessed the capricious moonlight; he did not wish to expose his delight in the case she were just being polite. "Bishop's Castle is hardly Shrewsbury proper, but it is close enough to visit whenever one chooses."

She seemed to hesitate for a moment before she spoke again. "Is it a very large house?"

There was no restraining his smile of delight at her leading question. "Large enough to have sheltered generations of Williams' for more than a hundred years. Currently I share it with my mother who is famous throughout the county for her gentle ways and unparalleled kindness."

"She sounds absolutely lovely," Mrs. Crenshaw said in a voice that, in his ears, sounded rather wistful.

"She is, indeed. I have found there are few women who can compare. I have not given up looking, however," he added and dared to place his free hand to cover hers where it lay on his arm. She tilted her head up at that, but the night was, at that moment, too dark to read her expression. He prayed he had not presumed too much.

They had obtained the wrought iron fence that surrounded the graveyard, and just as Theo put his hand to the latch at the gate, a great gust of wind blew a cyclone of leaves into the air.

"Oh!" Mrs. Crenshaw said as she threw up a hand to cover her mouth only to gasp again when he pushed open the gate, and a cat, startled by the squeak of the hinges, streaked past them.

"You are not frightened, are you, Mrs. Crenshaw? We may turn about and return to the house if you wish."

"No. . .no, it's only that I am persuaded Lady Avery might have indeed seen something," Mrs. Crenshaw said as she glanced around the large area of leaning tombstones, their inscriptions winking in and out of sight as the breeze cast the shadows of numerous willow branches to and fro. She indicated a particularly dark and forbidding tomb. "It seems the perfect place for a ghost to appear."

He nodded his agreement. "It certainly feels far friendlier when the sun is shining. See, there is a bench across from the tomb. We might await this supposed ghost's appearance in some comfort."

She seemed hesitant, but when he took her gloved hand she came willingly. He seated her on the bench and proceeded to investigate the carving above the tomb's door. Removing his own glove, he ran his fingers over the deeply grooved letters until he was satisfied. "Yes, it seems that this is, indeed, the Crenshaw family tomb."

"But, of course it is," she said in tones so subdued he began to fear he had made a mistake in bringing her to such a place.

And then he knew. "Your husband is laid to rest here, is he not?"

She nodded. "As is his grandfather and one day his father. And Grandmama."

Cursing himself for a fool, he sought to make reparations. "Does it not give you pain to be here? We shall depart at once!"

"No, I wish to remain here. I. . .it is difficult to explain, but it is important that I not give in to sadness. Not tonight."

Theo allowed himself a moment of gratification at her words before pushing it aside. It would not do to fancy her words were spoken with him in mind. Yet, if it were possible, for her to care for his sole company as much as he longed for hers was his dearest wish. Indeed, to look upon her, frozen with some nameless emotion and pale as marble in her gray cloak, was to gaze upon a beautiful statue, one with which he could fill his vision for the rest of his life. Carefully weighing his words before he spoke, he took up a seat next to her on the bench. "It is not wrong to yet mourn your husband."

She sat with her head turned away from him for so long, he thought perhaps she did not intend to reply.

"Mrs. Crenshaw?" he prodded. And then, more gently, "Anne."

Quicker than a heartbeat, she turned to look up at him and smiled. "Thank you. I do so prefer being addressed as such. I am a very simple person, a circumstance that led to a great deal of suffering during the course of my marriage. I would have you know," she hastened to inform him, "it had naught to do with my husband. He was a good man who died too soon without even the satisfaction of an heir to soften his passing," she added with a sad smile. "No, it was my father-in-law who made my life so comfortless. Though I miss my husband, I am only too glad to leave that life behind. A thought that often leaves me conscience-stricken is that God took him so that I might be released from the Duke's tyranny."

"You must never say so." He took her hand and gave it a gentle squeeze. "God takes whom He pleases, when He pleases, with little regard for our wishes. If it were not so, would there not be many deaths simply because it was convenient to someone or other?"

He was relieved to hear her soft chuckle. "Yes, I suppose that could be true."

"Yet, you are still troubled about something." He gave her hand another squeeze, though it felt incredibly rash to be possessed of it still.

"I expect it has something to do with feeling. . .unworthy. I can't quite credit the notion that I might deserve to be happy," she said with another smile meant for none but him.

Theo felt this to be a most pronounced indication of her possible feelings, however, just as he decided it to be an opportune moment to learn more, she gasped and jumped to her feet.

"What was that? It looked like a man standing— just there." She pointed to the entrance of the tomb, but Theo could see naught but shadows.

"Let us both be very still as we look in that direction," he suggested as he quelled his disappointment. They sat in breathless silence for longer than was comfortable. Then, just when he con-cluded that her ghost sighting was simply a means of preventing his speaking out of turn, he saw a man materialize right in front of his eyes. Anne stiffened beside him as Theo noted every detail of the man's appearance. He wore a rolled wig, a frock coat that came almost to his knees and a waistcoat nearly as long. His shoes were high and buckled; his stockings clocked, and his held a tricorn hat under his arm. "Who do you suppose he is?" he asked in hushed tones.

"I haven't the slightest idea nor do I wish to know," she replied in a low voice. "I am suddenly quite cold. Would you be so kind as to escort me back to the house?"

"But of course!" He helped her to her feet and turned for one last look at the ghost—but it had gone.

Chapter Three

$\mathcal{A}$nne had never been so frightened in all her life. Not for one moment had she believed a genuine ghost should be found in the graveyard at Dunsmere, or any other, for that matter. She had never before considered whether or not she believed in specters, but she was now persuaded she did not, at least, had not before tonight. "Mr. Williams, I believe it would be best not to inform Lady Avery of what we have seen. That is to say, what we *think* we have seen. She is of a very excitable nature, and I fear if we were to describe our experience, it would only create an intolerable commotion."

"I could not agree more, Mrs., that is; Anne, and you shall call me Theo."

He must have felt how she shivered for he put his arm around her shoulders and pulled her close to his side as they walked the path back to the ball. The house blocked much of the wind, and the air warmed as they drew closer. The glow from the windows as well as the flambeaux that lined the broad drive restored her to her to a sense of comfort far too routine to entertain thoughts of ghosts on the premises; it now seemed quite impossible.

As it was early enough that none had thought of departing the ball, the entrance to the manse was deserted, and they were quite alone. Suddenly she recalled what had been her expectations when she first agreed to hold vigil in the graveyard and was taken aback at how keen was her disappointment. She must find a way to prolong their privacy so as to give Mr. Williams a chance to speak before Grandmama sent him home.

"Theo," she said as naturally as if she said it every day of her life, "I do believe I have seen that face before. He looked very much like a man in the portrait gallery. Could it be that I made up the ghost out of whole cloth?"

"I saw him, as well, do not forget. What if we were to take a look at the portrait? If he resembles the man we each saw we shall know it could not have been pure imagination on either of our parts."

"Yes, of course, what a splendid idea!" Anne enthused as if he hadn't plucked the very thought from her own mind. "First thing in the morning after breakfast we shall go and see what can be learned."

They had neared the massive portals of Dunsmere but, Theo, his arm still about her, seemed to hesitate. He stopped and turned her round so that she faced him as he placed one large, warm hand on each of her shoulders. "Anne, do you suppose the Dowager will allow me to stay on another day? I rather suspect she has only been tolerating me until the ball has concluded."

Anne felt a pain prick her heart at the thought of his departure. "I have feared the same, but I truly cannot say what she shall decide. She is full of whims and fancies." Though Anne knew it to be selfish, she enjoyed the way his face fell at her words.

"Do you suppose we might have a look at the portrait tonight? Surely we might slip away again."

Anne nodded in agreement though she rather doubted Grandmama would countenance a second desertion from the ball. There was Her Grace's son, the Duke, with whom to be reckoned, as well. If only Mr. Williams would speak. Should he declare himself and Anne accept him, Grandmama could hardly send him away, not just yet. However, it was not to be. He took her hand

and led her to the house and through the doors to rejoin the ball, the remainder of which was a bit of a daze. She did have one waltz with Theo, but it seemed highly unsatisfactory after their time alone earlier in the evening. She supposed it was just a nonsensical notion but it seemed her father-in-law never took his eyes from her, and she agonized over which impropriety she was committing that he should frown at her so.

Once her waltz with Theo was over, she did not lack for partners, one of whom was the daunting Marquis of Trevelin. The only circumstance that overshadowed the unpleasantness of his scarred mouth was his unsavory reputation. As a debutante nearly a decade past, Anne was thoroughly warned away from him. She thought it all of a piece to be waltzing in his arms in the same hour she had seen her first phantom and suspected his request for a set was at the behest of the Duke who *would* insist on meddling in her affairs even when not under his roof. Theo was quite in demand, as well, but she knew to credit his dancing every set to his impeccable manners and quiet charm. In the end, there wasn't the opportunity to slip away with him to inspect the painting in the portrait gallery.

Quite late in the evening, as she made her way through the throngs of people in order to find a moment to recover from the overwhelming heat, she found herself quitting the room in train with the Duke and his nephew, Sir Anthony. Just ahead of them was the Duchess and Lady Crenshaw who looked at daggers drawn. She eschewed the odious habit of eavesdropping, but she was more than a little curious as to what the disagreement could be about. Surely, she should not be held accountable for any words that reached her ears of their own accord.

"I do believe we should affiance my son to your daughter," the Duke pronounced with a smile so smug and wide even Anne could see it from her position just behind his shoulder.

"I haven't a daughter," Sir Anthony replied with a cat-in-the-cream pot smile of his own.

"That is as it may be. Nevertheless, you one day shall," His Grace returned as if privy to future events unknown by any but God.

"I thank you for the honor, but I am persuaded the idea appeals to the Duchess not at all."

"No, I suppose it does not."

"Am I right, then, in thinking you enjoy causing her discomfort?" Sir Anthony asked in obvious surprise. As for Anne, she was not in the least astonished.

"What I enjoy," the Duke purred, "is witnessing my wife's delight at the discomfort of yours."

With those words, the Duchess spun around and, in a voice loud enough for Anne to hear, announced her view on the matter. "Just think, we are to be in-laws to one another's children!"

Anne thought Lady Crenshaw not in the least grateful for the honor as her face turned sheet-white. She, however, said nothing, a lack of response that seemed to drive the Duchess wild. With a smile that showed every one of her teeth, she took her husband by the arm and led him quickly away.

The exchange deepened Anne's desire to be free of the Duke and his sway over her. A week ago she would never have countenanced so much as the contemplation of marriage, but that was before she had met Theodore Williams, a man so gentle and kind that she have need have no fear he would treat her with anything but honor. Moreover, unlike her husband, Theo would surely stand up for her, protect her and indulge her wishes. The fact that his smile spread to his eyes so that they twinkled like stars and her heart beat a bit faster at the sight of him was a sure sign that they should suit. However, barring a glance or two of him on the dance floor, she did not see him again for the remainder of the ball.

It was not the least unreasonable to assume he very well might be gone shortly after breakfast in the morning. As such, she climbed the stairs to her bedchamber with a heavy heart. She walked as slowly as possible to her door down the passageway in hopes he would magically appear at one end or the other as did the ghost in the graveyard. He did not. With great reluctance, she opened the door to her room and crossed the threshold feeling precisely as if she were sealing her fate, one that did not include Theo Williams. It took all of her courage to close the door behind her, whereupon, she sat at the dressing table and burst into tears.

Finally, exhausted and spent, she began to remove the jewels from her hair and was startled by a knock at her door. It proved to be the maid who had readied her for the ball and had come to help Anne out of her beautiful ball gown on which she had pinned so many hopes. She then helped Anne to don a night rail, blew out the bedside candle and silently departed. Too worn out even to cry herself to sleep, Anne closed her eyes and prayed for she knew not what.

She thought perhaps she had dozed a bit before a gentle knock roused her. She could scarcely imagine what the maid might have forgotten and hurried to open the door without lighting a candle or donning a wrap. "What is it?" she asked as she pulled the door wide.

There stood Mr. Williams *sans* shoes or jacket, a candle in his hand and a finger to his lips.

"Mr. Williams!" she hissed in disapproval whilst her heart leapt with unbridled joy. In the glow of the candle, his shadow climbed even taller than he and his eyes looked black yet the most tender she had ever seen them.

"Her Grace has given me my conge."

Anne felt the tears start in her eyes but refused to give them free reign. "I am so very sorry, Theo. It is good of you to tell me. I shall arise extra early for breakfast. I do so enjoy our breakfasts together," she said, her voice faltering.

"I should be most distressed if you rose early on my account; dawn is but a few hours away."

"Oh," she said, the sudden pain in her chest threatening to rob her of breath. "Then, I shall not see you again?"

"It would seem not. Would you. . .Would you come with me?" he asked as he held out his hand to her.

"Go with you? But where?" She knew she should immediately slam the door between herself and temptation but found she simply could not.

"Only to the portrait gallery. We must identify our ghost at the very least."

"Yes, oh yes, of course!" She felt greatly relieved that his intentions were thoroughly innocent and indulged herself in a moment of speculation; how his eyes should have twinkled if he had guessed the thoughts that crossed her mind! "I shall just be a moment." She flew to find something with which to cover her night rail and came away with the peacock blue shawl which she wrapped firmly about herself. Going again to the door, she took the hand he held out still and quietly shut the door behind her.

She had moved down the passageways of Dunsmere in near darkness on more than one occasion and had never felt even a flicker of fear. However, in spite of the warmth of Theo's hand clasping her own, she could not help but feel as if peril lingered in the depths of each and every shadow. "I cannot rightly recall; are apparitions tied to one place or might they appear anywhere?" she asked in a voice that, much to her chagrin, quavered. "I do believe I shall scream if a ghost appears right before our very eyes." She shivered and leaned in closer to Theo who responded by putting his arm around her shoulders.

"I am far from an authority on the subject, but I am persuaded I have heard tell of ghosts who have appeared according to their will. However, you mustn't scream; someone shall hear you."

"Yes, of course, you are most correct." She put a hand to her mouth to suppress any whimpering of a spontaneous nature and forced herself to go on until they reached the staircase. "The gallery is down this flight and on the far side of the ballroom. Do be careful of this step, just here," she advised, "as it will squeak if you do not tread upon it lightly."

"I fear I am much too much man to tread on any step lightly," he bantered as the step did, indeed, creak under the weight of the tallest man Anne had ever before met. She had always fancied she would feel overshadowed in the presence of such a giant and was a bit taken aback by how sheltered, guarded and cherished it made her feel. It would all be of no consequence after tonight as he would be gone in a matter of hours, most likely never to return. The thought filled her with a fear far greater than that induced by the ghost and she willed away the tears that started in her eyes.

When they made it down the stairs with no one the wiser that they were abroad in the night, she sighed her relief. She led him down the hall, through the blackened ballroom that had been a beacon of light only an hour since, and through to the portrait gallery which ran the length of the house. She couldn't be certain but felt the painting in question was on the far end. Theo held up his candle to inspect the portraits in the case she was wrong and, as they passed each one, Anne's apprehension grew. What if the face in the painting were the same as the one in the graveyard? The very idea caused a ripple of alarm to run up her spine so that her entire body shivered.

He drew her closer as if he felt her shuddering, and they made their way down the lengthy gallery. When they reached the end, Anne knew the last painting, a full-length one with a gold frame of a magnificence that surpassed even its enormity, was the one for which they had been looking. Theo held up the candle so that the visage of the man pictured should be plain to both and Anne was instantly gripped with a chill from head to toe. It was, indeed, the same man with the very same long, pointed nose and deep-set eyes under the very same rolled wig, old-fashioned frock coat and buckled shoes.

"Theo, is it the man you saw?" she whispered.

"Yes," he replied in a voice that registered both resignation and a tinge of surprise. "I assume I am not wrong to suppose he is the one you saw, as well?"

She nodded, too shocked to speak. It was then that the glow of a distant light caught the corner of her eye, and she turned to see a ball of fire advance so slowly towards them that it seemed almost to stand still. She felt Theo's shock in the arm he had about her shoulders and wordlessly, they watched the ball grow larger and larger until, quite suddenly, it was upon them.

"I see you have met the infamous Duke," came a voice from behind the flames, one so dry and thin it took a moment for Anne to recognize it as the Dowager's.

"Grandmama!" she cried.

The Dowager's face appeared from behind the brace of glowing candles she held aloft as she turned to view the portrait. "We never did meet in this life. He was my husband's sire, but he died rather young, just as did his son after him, and my own. They say he walks this house and the grounds beyond, and many have heard him, including myself, I am sorry to say." She turned to regard them, her eyes black as wells of ink in her skull. "However, he rarely appears and only as a warning at times of great danger," she said in so ominous a manner that Anne felt herself shiver with apprehension.

"What are you saying?" Anne asked. "Is someone to die? A person in this house?"

The Dowager appeared to consider Anne's question for a bit before she spoke. "It is not as simple as all that. He warns against actions, so much like his own, choices that will lead to any manner of peril. It is said that he atones for the sins of his youth by warning his descendants. As of yet, not one of them has heeded his message."

"Does he speak, then?" Theo queried. "What manner of warning does he give?"

"He never speaks. His appearance is enough. Doubtless, that is why my son the Duke shall take no notice, just as his father and uncles failed to do."

"But, how are we to know the warning is for the Duke of Marcross? Can it not be for anyone in the house?" Anne asked. "Does his appearance always presage certain death?"

"Who is to say?" the Dowager replied with a shrug of her shoulder. "However, he has appeared prior to the death of my husband, each of his three brothers and, I am sorry to say, my beloved son."

"Not Uncle John!" Anne cried before she thought better of it. "I beg your pardon, Grandmama, but Reed often spoke of how dissimilar John was from the rest of the Crenshaws."

"Yes, as different as Anthony is from his uncle, but he required a warning as much as the rest. He had a weak heart, but he refused to drink less, ride less, and he kept the most appalling hours. I was grief-stricken when he died, just as did the rest of them who deserved it far more."

Anne was overcome with a new fear. "Reed; you don't mean that he. . .?"

"Yes, as a warning of what was to come but not to anyone who knew to mention it until it was too late. Needless to say, a ghost that refuses to speak has little hope of comprehension. I only understood it after the accident, myself. I made inquiries," the Dowager added in so low a voice, Anne nearly did not catch her words.

"It would seem this ghost is not particularly discerning," Theo pointed out. "To whom did he come the last time?"

The Dowager looked at him in some surprise. "To you, if I am to trust my instincts."

"Yes, Grandmama, you are most correct, but, I believe Mr. Williams desires to know to whom the ghost appeared prior to tonight."

"It is of no consequence," the Dowager said with a wave of her hand. "It clearly has no bearing on his message. If he can appear to that witless Lady Avery, he clearly has, as you say, Mr. Williams, no discernment. That he appears, is enough."

Anne had many more questions but her resolution dissolved when Theo drew her closer into the circle of his arm. She felt such comfort in his touch that she knew she need fear nothing as long as he was near.

"Your Grace," he stated, "I can see you are apprehensive about this ghost. How you must agonize that one of your family is in danger. I don't believe there is any reason to fear Anne could possibly be the one for whom the ghost appeared, but I shall not quit this house until I am persuaded she is not."

Anne knew her emotions to be her downfall as she felt them quiver between her own fears and a giddy joy. "Oh, yes, Grandmama! I do believe I shall feel much safer were Mr. Williams present; at least until we learn what is meant by the ghost's appearance," she pleaded.

"I do believe I shall, as well," the Dowager said to Anne's astonishment. "I shall give you, Mr. Williams, free reign to ask what you might of whom. If there is an ill fate awaiting my son the Duke, so be it, but if my Anthony is in danger, I shall move Heaven and Earth to put a stop to it!"

It seemed there was nothing more to say and the three of them moved, as one, down the long gallery and back the way they had come. Not a word was exchanged, but Anne dared to put a hand to rest against Theo's where it encircled her shoulder. Periodically he gave it a squeeze as he looked down into her face with a light in his eyes that owed nothing to the candle he held.

Once they had climbed the stairs and headed down the passage of private chambers, Anne began to feel apprehensive. Not only should she be required to spend the balance of the night alone in her room but Grandmama would likely make some humiliating remark designed to keep Theo at arm's length. However, when they gained her door, she disappeared into her room with nary a word.

Anne looked at Theo in astonishment who gazed back at her in such a way that it would surely have made the blood sing in her veins if she hadn't been so stiff with fear. "I shall see you at breakfast, as usual," she related. "Afterwards, we shall begin our quest for answers."

He gave no response until he had dropped his arm from her shoulder and stepped round to tower over her. "I am just down the hall. You need only scream, and I shall be at your door."

"Yes. Yes, I do know. Thank you. It is a comfort."

"You are trembling. Is it just with cold?"

"Yes," she said but she saw in his eyes that he knew she lied.

"What if I were to stay?"

Anne felt the shock in her face. "Whatever can you mean, Mr. Williams?"

"Now, now, don't jump to conclusions. I merely suggest that I might sit here, outside your door, and you might sit on the other side. I expect you are too frightened to sleep, and you should not be alone. Dawn won't be long in coming; we can wait it out together."

"Why, Mr. Williams, what a brilliant notion," Anne replied with as much enthusiasm as she could manage without the Dowager overhearing.

"What is this 'Mr. Williams'?" he asked in extravagant dismay. "I had thought we were more than comfortable with Theo."

"Yes, I am. That is; I had thought so, as well," she added in hopes she had not given away too much of her feelings. "Shall we try it, then? We shall have to whisper so that Grandmama does not hear us."

"In that case," he said as he turned the key, pushed open her chamber door and indicated that she should enter, "perhaps we might leave the door open, just a crack, so as to hear one another without disturbing Her Grace."

Anne felt they were skating perilously close to dangerous territory but did not hesitate to fetch Theo a blanket from the bed. They sat as he suggested, he with her blanket and she with another, as they went over the trivia of their respective lives, childhoods and wishes for the future, the door open just enough that they might see one another's face in the glow of his candle. The time passed as if it were nothing, and the sun's rays made their way into their dark and comfortable cose far too soon. When Anne could fully discern Theo's face, she knew it was time to bid one another adieu for the time being.

"I am forever in your debt, Theo, but the maid will soon be up to light the fires and I had best be found beneath the covers when she does."

He rose and passed the blanket through to her with an angelic smile of gratitude that was thoroughly undone by the devilish twinkle in his eye. However, somewhat to her dismay, his words were perfectly innocent. "You must promise to lay abed until you feel rested. The later we commence our ghost hunt, the longer it shall take." He took her hand and held it in the space that marked the threshold. "I, for one, am eager for it to take as long as possible."

Anne felt herself blush. "I had never supposed I should be so glad to have seen a ghost," she said, hoping desperately that her words communicated her own eagerness without compromising the last of her decorum.

He said nothing but the expression in his eyes spoke volumes. He stepped closer, drew her hand to his lips and kissed it. "Goodnight, Anne."

She wanted nothing more than to prolong the moment, to discover in what direction it might lead, what else might have been said to indicate the state of his feelings, but there wasn't the time. Regretfully she withdrew her hand and pushed to the door as gently as possible. As she wrapped herself in the blanket that had so recently warmed the tall but tender man with whom she had shared her dreams, she contemplated the happiness she might find in life, if only it included Theo. With a sigh, she returned to bed and was asleep before the maid scratched at the door.

When she awoke, the room was sunk in the shadows of high noon. Quickly, she rose and dressed for the day. Though she wished to lengthen the time Theo spent at Dunsmere as much as he, she had no desire to waste even a moment of it away from him.

Chapter Four

Theo sat in the breakfast room, polishing off the remains of a sumptuous feast. He had slept less than he ought but longer than he had wished. He meant to make the most of his time with Anne and he meant to begin as soon as possible. When she came through the door, looking delightfully disheveled, he thought, perhaps, she felt the same.

Leaping to his feet, he pulled out a chair. "What shall you have to break your fast this lovely morning? Or is it already the afternoon?" he gently chided as he went to the sideboard and took up a plate. "We have ghostly kippers, phantom eggs and an alarming lack of banshee bacon."

Anne laughed, a thoroughly enchanting sound. "I had best have as much banshee bacon as remains. I am persuaded every successful ghost hunt courts disaster if not fortified with plentiful bacon and eggs and a rack of demon toast with bloodied butter."

He ladled the food onto her plate as she spoke and set it before her as he took up his seat. "Where, then, shall we start? I do believe we have had all the information we might hope to obtain from the Dowager. Which, then, are the servants who have been at the house the longest?"

"An excellent notion, Mr. Williams," she said in bantering tones as she started in on a slice of toast. "Perhaps I should corner the cook whilst you head out to the stables to speak with the groom."

This was not what Theo had in mind. "I had thought perhaps we might conduct our investigation together. Surely we might corner the cook *ensemble*. Suppose we request an audience on account of the sad state of the phantom eggs?"

"That would be a place to start," she said, giving those on her fork a dubious look. "When we are through with her I am persuaded by tomorrow we might expect more banshee bacon than we can manage."

"You wound me! You slept so long I had naught to do but ruminate on the bacon. Proper punishment shall follow accordingly; try as you might you shall not shake me. Not only shall the cook fall prey to our combined interrogative efforts but so shall the groom, the boot boy and the gardener."

Anne joined her cup with its saucer and chuckled her appreciation. "If only you had risen even earlier and had breakfast at a decent hour, you needn't have eaten enough for luncheon, as well!"

Ah, but if I had, I should have been cooling my heels in the drawing room with none but the Dowager with whom to pass the time," he said as he pulled Anne's chair away from the table and assisted her to stand. "Shall we brave the denizens of the kitchen?"

"I so hope they do not feel invaded," Anne remarked as she put her hand through his arm and set a companionable pace for the nether regions of the house. "I am persuaded I should be most put out if a guest in the house were suddenly to appear in my kitchen with questions about the family and anything as nonsensical as ghosts. Do you suppose any shall know a thing, and if so will they feel free to share it?"

"All we can do is ask," he said as he pushed open the green baize door that separated the main house from the domain of the servants. They encountered a few startled maids who hastily put their heads down and scurried on their way, but none dared to stop them, so they pressed on to the kitchen. As they hadn't an idea whom the cook might be, they made inquiries until they found themselves in her austere presence.

"Mrs. Preston," Theo began, interpreting Anne's silence as reticence to broach any subject at all whatsoever with the intimidating cook. "We wished to express our congratulations on a delicious breakfast, only, we thought the eggs a bit clammy."

"Oh!" Anne cried as if this was woeful news of which she had been unaware. "I believed it to be the paucity of bacon that brought us here this morning."

"The what of what?" Mrs. Preston demanded with a penetrating glare for each of them. "I will have you know I supplied the breakfast room with an entire rack of rashers."

"I do beg your pardon," he said with a long look for Anne whose eyes sparkled with mirth. "Someone must have eaten it all before I came down."

This bit of prevarication led Anne to stifle a snort of laughter behind one fine-boned hand, an action that prevented her from taking in the look of disapproval bestowed upon her by Mrs. Preston.

"I shall see that there is more tomorrow morning, Sir. Will that be all?" she asked in so stiff a manner that Theo fleetingly considered abating her indignation with a buss to the cheek. However, in the end, he felt it safest to plunge on to the matter at hand.

"That would be most satisfactory, Mrs. Preston, and many thanks. There is, however, another matter. Her Grace has given Mrs. Crenshaw and I leave to conduct an inquiry into the matter of the resident ghost. Have you seen it?" he asked in hopes he did not sound as foolish as he felt.

Suddenly, a loud crash came from behind. Anne gasped as they whirled to discover that an enormous platter had fallen from its place in the Welsh cupboard. A pair of kitchen maids scurried to clear up the mess as they tried, in vain, to hide their terror.

"Is this a frequent occurrence?" Theo wondered aloud.

The cook only stared back at him from a face distinguished by overly-round eyes and a triple row of chins.

"Do you not find it odd that the platter fell at the precise moment we asked about the ghost?"

"No, I do not," the cook replied in a voice cold enough to form icicles in hell.

"I see," he said with a conciliatory smile, then turned, eyebrows raised, to favor Anne with a look of incredulity.

"Have you not seen the ghost, Mrs. Preston?" Anne asked, far more kindly than Theo felt was deserved.

"I have not and would thank you to refrain from spooking the staff with such barmy notions."

"Oh!" Anne said, distressed. "But we do have leave from Grandmama to ask about it."

As this speech made no impression on Mrs. Preston, Theo concluded it was time to end the interview. "We won't trouble you any longer," he said as he slipped Anne's hand into his with a squeeze and held it out of sight of the formidable cook. "However, if any of your staff has something to relay, please send him or her to us as soon as possible."

Mrs. Preston looked dubious as to her willingness to comply, but she nodded curtly before turning her back to them and proceeding about her day.

"Well then!" Theo said. "I believe we have done enough ghost-hunting for one day. Let's go for a ride, shall we?" he asked with another squeeze to her hand, so soft and small in his. She favored him with a sweet smile, one that seemed full of promise, and his heart turned over in his chest.

"I shall just go change into my habit," she said, putting her arm through his and gazing up into his eyes. "And, perhaps, afterward we might visit the circulating library again. I am persuaded they shall have a book or two on specters and spooks."

Theo covered her hand where it lay on his arm and considered himself the most fortunate of men. His good opinion
of his fortuity only strengthened as they spent the remainder
of the morning and the afternoon together. They took their
time with their ride and dismounted to walk, hand in hand,
through the meadow that verged the gates at the far side of the
estate. At the library, they found an illustrated volume depict-
ing various phantoms and apparitions adorned with sheets
over which they giggled until tears came to their eyes. They
stopped to join some children in a game of lawn bowls on the
village green and stepped into the local drapers so as to allow
Anne the requisite ribbons and a new pair of riding of gloves,
long overdue.

The Dowager absented herself from dinner; a meal made
merrier for the dearth of caustic remarks and looks of disdain
and, afterwards, they retired to the drawing room, Anne by the
fire and he across the room where he surreptitiously might
take in the effect of her profile against the flames. He wondered if she possibly could have an accurate perception of her
beauty; how her eyes turned to mulberry wine and her hair
to burnished gold in the light of the fire. He felt it the ideal
moment to speak but wasn't entirely sure she would be willing to tether herself to marriage so soon. However, nothing
short of an expeditious marriage would do; now that he had
found her, he intended to never spend a day deprived of her
presence. He cleared his throat and opened his mouth, but his
gentle voicing of her name was drowned out by the sound of
a knocking at the door.

Anne jerked as if feeling a strain not apparent in her manner
until that moment. She looked to him with eyes round with apprehension. When a kitchen maid entered, her shoulders dropped in
relief, and he realized she had misgivings with regard to the coming hours of dark solitude.

"Sor, beggin' your pardon, Sor," the maid said, bobbing a curtsey. "Mrs. Preston said as we should come to you if we had summit to say about the ghost hereabouts."

"What is it?" Anne asked in a hollow voice. "What do you know?"

I ha'n't seen him for myself, Missus, i'were me aunt who worked here afore me."

"May we speak to her, then?" Theo asked.

"No, Sor, she died of the consumption. But she knew it were comin', Sor, on account o' the ghost."

He looked to Anne to gage her reaction and quickly shook his head to convey his rejection of the maid's story. "Surely, you don't feel the ghost came for your aunt?"

"Thot's just wot she said afore she died, Sor. That the ghost had come like he had afore and that she was to die."

Theo looked again to Anne and, registering her anxiety, hesitated to allow the girl to speak further. However, Anne rose to her feet and, to his surprise, began to pepper the maid with questions.

"Where did your aunt see the ghost? Did he say anything? What made her believe it was her death he foresaw?"

The maid, her brow wrinkled as she turned the questions over in her mind, hesitated a bit before answering. "Come to think on't, I don't know that she said where she saw it. And, no he said naught that I know of. I suppose she thot t'was her meant to die on account of she was the one that saw him."

"But your aunt died of consumption, did she not?"

"Yes, Sor, she did, that very night, right after telling me mum that she had seen the old duke appear."

"Thank you, that will be all," Theo said a bit more curtly than he ought. The girl had come according to his desire and had told him exactly what he had asked to know; he should not lay Anne's increasing trepidation at the girl's door. However, the moment she had departed he took Anne into his arms and attempted to ease her fears. "Her aunt suffered from illness, doubtless, for years before it finally took her. The ghost did not come for her; she would have died at any rate."

"Yes, but she did die and so soon after seeing the ghost!" she said as she pushed away from him to better look up into his eyes. "Perhaps he came to warn her just as he has warned us."

"Hush, now," he crooned as he pulled her head tightly against his chest and stroked her hair. "Neither of us are ill nor likely to soon die of old age."

"We should not ride, Theo," she said, her voice faint and muffled in the voluminous folds of his cravat. "Riding is dangerous. One of us might take a fall."

"Then we shan't. I do think you have no cause to worry, but we may effortlessly avoid riding if it pleases you."

"Yes, Theo, it pleases me very much. And the carriage," she said, tilting her head back to watch his expression. "We shan't need it for anything tomorrow, should you think? We have just been to town."

Looking down into her eyes, he wanted nothing more than to cover her mouth with his own. However, her profound anxiety coupled with the difference in their heights prevented him. "Come, Anne, let us sit by the fire and think on what we should do." He led her to the wingback chair closest to the flames, seated himself and, despite her feeble protests, drew her down into his lap.

With a sigh, she settled her head against his collarbone so that it fitted just under his chin, and slowly, the tension eased from her arms and shoulders. They sat in silence for some time, and when he felt that her fear had sufficiently abated, he took both of her dainty hands in his own and tightened his hold around her with the other. As he bent his head to look into her face, his heart suddenly took up a pounding he was persuaded could be detected in the next room. She gave no sign that anything was amiss, however, but looked up to stare at him, her eyes glowing like stars of amethyst.

"Anne, I. . ." he began but was cut off by her horrified exclamation.

"Grandmama!"

"Where?" he cried and all but discarded Anne from his lap in his dismay.

"Upstairs! Don't you recall?" she asked, too overwrought to notice his dread of having been discovered by the Dowager with Anne in his lap. "She was not well. That is why she did not come down to dinner. Oh, Theo, what if the ghost were meant for her?"

At the moment, he could have happily consigned Her Grace to her heavenly abode, or worse, but felt it best to refrain from saying so. "She is an old woman. I am persuaded she simply needs her rest."

"You are right, of course, but Theo," she said as she rose and began to pace the floor. "I find I cannot be composed until I know how she fares."

Theo drew a deep breath and let it out in a silent sigh. "If you think it best, then of course you must go to her."

"I do, and if she is feeling poorly yet, I think I must sit up with her tonight," she added as she wrung her beautiful hands in consternation.

"I think that a splendid scheme." Though he would have rathered share a seat by the fire with Anne for many hours yet, he suspected it was a pointless ambition. Clearly, she had no desire to spend the night alone in her room, and he hadn't the heart to deprive her of a plausible excuse. "I suppose this is goodnight, then," he said, rising to his feet and taking her hand. "Tomorrow we shall stay close to home and learn whatever else remains to be learned."

"Thank you, Theo! I don't know what I should do without you," she said, her hand warm and supple in his and her eyes, so very soft and tender.

In that moment, he knew she would say yes if he offered her marriage. Instead, he watched her walk away from him, every one of his muscles yearning to go after her, to take her in his arms and kiss her hair, her face, her lips, until she forgot Grandmama, the tiresome ghost, her dead husband and all other cares other than Theodore Williams. In spite of his wishes, she had somehow quit the room and closed the door behind her, leaving him with nothing but his thoughts and the chair in which they had been together. Slowly, he sat and positioned himself as he had been, the imaginary head under his chin just as real as mere minutes prior, the weight of her slim body against his right arm just as vibrant, closed his eyes and dreamed of the morrow.

Theo woke to find himself in his bed and slow to remember the events of the night previous. Gradually, his head began to clear as the room filled with light until, suddenly, he realized it was the day he would, without fail, ask Anne to be his wife. He hurried down to breakfast, sure he would find her prepared to do battle with him over the bacon, but she was not there.

He rang for the maid and learned that Anne was still with the Dowager, and the doctor had been sent for. It seemed he was to spend the day on his own but rather than give in to disappointment he determined to make more inquiries. He was now convinced that the sooner he might solve the mystery of the ghost the sooner Anne should fully turn her attention to Theo.

He decided to begin with the gardener as the ghost had last been seen on the grounds. Perhaps he had appeared there the time before, as well. Prior to leaving the house, he filled a plate with Anne's favorite foodstuffs, including a generous portion of perfectly cooked bacon, and left instructions that it should be taken up to her. Then he went in search of answers.

Baldwin, the gardener, was found raking leaves out of the flower beds that fronted the entrance to the chapel grounds. As Theo approached, the gardener raised his head and pushed back his hat to reveal an expression that suggested questions would not be welcomed. Theo, however, refused to be daunted and held out his hand for the gardener to shake.

"I am Mr. Williams, a guest staying at the house."

The gardener shook Theo's hand and gave a curt nod.

"I have been enjoying the excellent grounds," Theo said with a look that took in the vast lawns, overflowing flower beds and immaculate rose garden. "I am persuaded there is not a better man with a spade this side of the Continent." To Theo's surprise, this fulsome compliment failed to soften the gardener's expression one whit. "Ah, well, I suppose I should come to the point. Her Grace has given me carte blanche to ask questions with regard to the resident ghost."

Baldwin raised his brows so far his hat rose into the air. "I don't know that you would call it a resident. It hasn't ever appeared in the house."

"Then, you *have* seen it?"

Baldwin renewed his grip on his rake and returned to his work. "How could I?" he protested. "No such thing as ghosts."

Theo was of the same opinion, yet, he and Anne had seen something; he was not about to give up until he could assure her that all would be well. "Pray tell, how does one see a ghost when such does not exist?"

The gardener shrugged. "Imagination? Hysteria? Who can say?"

Though Theo had yet to experience a single moment of hysteria in his life, he was willing to attribute his ghost sighting to imagination. He had believed the face of the man in the portrait to be the same as that he had seen in the graveyard, but it was certainly not evidence of a conclusive nature. Theo had seen many such portraits; one darkened visage graced with a needled nose was much like the other.

"You have never heard tell of the ghost being seen anywhere than the graveyard?" The gardener shook his head and Theo pressed on. "What of the platter falling to the floor the moment we inquired about the ghost from the cook?"

"What of it?"

"Well, is that known to happen on a regular basis, perhaps when a door is opened or closed somewhere in the house?"

The gardener lifted his foot to tamp down a bit of disturbed dirt and looked up at Theo with a wry smile. "Seems as if you have all the answers with no aid from me."

"That is fair. But what of the kitchen maid's aunt? She died the very night she saw the ghost."

"Did she, now?" The gardener's tone was dubious.

"Well, didn't she?"

"She died; that much is true."

"It was of the consumption, I've been told."

"Who knows what one imagines when in the grip of the consumption?" Baldwin mused.

Theo was hard-pressed to formulate a reply. Though he felt all of his questions had been answered, he knew Anne would need more. "Her Grace's granddaughter, Mrs. Crenshaw; she has been overwrought since she saw what she believed to be a ghost. What should I say to her?"

Baldwin allowed his rake to fall to the ground and turned to fully face Theo. "She saw this supposed ghost at, what—close on midnight?"

"Yes, I do believe it was."

"Well, then, I can't make no promises as the moon won't be as full tonight as it t'were then, but if you bring her close onto the same hour, I will do my best to explain your ghost."

Theo wasn't the least satisfied that such a thing could be done, but he once again shook the gardener's hand and thanked him. As he turned to walk towards the house, there came the rattle of wheels on the road and Baldwin sprinted to the front gate to allow a carriage to enter. Suspecting it was the doctor, Theo proceeded to make himself least in sight in the library until he could draw the physician aside upon his departure. As such, Theo spent an anxious quarter hour as he waited for his chance to learn what conclusions were being drawn above stairs.

If the Dowager was, indeed, dying, Theo was persuaded Anne should prove inconsolable. Yet, if the Dowager suffered from a harmless complaint, Anne wasn't likely to suffer any less foreboding; it should only prove to change focus. When he spotted her descending the stairs with the doctor, her expression peaceful and her eyes alight as she caught sight of him waiting for her, he felt a weight lift from his shoulders.

"Theo, you will be relieved to know that Grandmama suffers from a simple cold. She will doubtless be up and about on the morrow. Is that not wonderful?"

"Yes, it is," he replied with a smile that might have seemed a bit broad for such innocuous news. To Theo, however, there was nothing of the banal with regard to having Anne to himself for the rest of the day and evening. With the Dowager abed, it should prove far easier to take Anne for a midnight walk for their final ghost hunt, as well. Together they bid the doctor adieu, whereupon Theo ushered Anne into the library and shut the door behind him.

"You are looking more yourself. How is Grandmama?"

"She is fine, Theo, truly she is. I feel a bit foolish for having been in such a taking over her."

"I am very glad to hear it, for there is something I should like to say to you."

"And I should love to hear it, but I most go to Grandmama. She is miserable and has asked that I read to her so as to pass the time."

She must have seen his dismay at her words for she rushed to reassure him. "We shall see one another at dinner, Theo. Can that not be soon enough?

"I suppose it must do. However, you must promise to give me your full attention when once I have you to myself again."

She smiled and laid her hand upon his arm. "Of course you shall have it."

"And if I require that you go for a midnight stroll with me, you shall do as I ask?"

Her smile brightened. "I am looking forward to it."

As she quit the room, Theo swore that it should be the last time she walked away from him unspoken for. The hours until the evening meal seemed without end, and when, at dinnertime, instead of Anne, he received a note explaining her continued absence, he thought his lot could not have been more difficult to bear. She finally met him in the drawing room, quite late, after the Dowager had finally fallen into a deep sleep.

"Oh, Theo, please do not glare at me so!" Anne pled as she went to him and put her hands in his. "Grandmama was in such a mood; I didn't wish to be ungrateful. It has been so good of her to allow me to stay here. And then there's you," she added, her voice growing softer. "She has allowed you to stay, as well, and I owe her much for that."

"As do I," he said with a gentle squeeze of her hands. "Now that this ghost business is done with, I fear she will finally have reason to turn me out."

"Whatever do you mean? If not for Grandmama, then for whom has the ghost come to warn us?"

"As to that," Theo said as he led her to the sofa and settled her next to him for a long cose, "there is much to tell you." With growing impatience, he related all he had learned about the ghost and his conclusions, wishing, all the while that they could be done with the whole subject and, at long last, make inroads as to the subject of their lives together.

"After we have learned what it is the gardener wishes to tell us, I have a question to ask of you. It must wait until then, but it shall not wait a moment past."

Anne blushed and looked down at her hands. He felt then that he had her answer, but he dared not presume too much. Time had passed far more quickly in her presence than the hours prior, and once the hall clock struck the hour of half past eleven, he sent her off to collect her cloak and meet him in the front hall. They walked down the drive, her arm through his and pressed tight to his side just as the night of the ball. It seemed difficult to believe that a mere two days had passed since then, one of them having been the happiest of his life.

They found Baldwin waiting for them in the graveyard by the tomb of the Crenshaws. When Anne spotted him, she looked a question at Theo, but he merely put a finger to his lips and gave the gardener leave to speak.

"Many people have claimed to see a ghost in this graveyard over the decades. Their accounts are so similar it easily could sway one to believe in its happenin'. In every event, save, perhaps, that of the dyin', hysterical maidservant, the ghost has been spotted at the entrance of this tomb. They are all adamant the ghost never speaks. Together, these two claims are what prove that the ghost is a figment of the imagination."

"Are you accusing me of hysteria, then?" Anne inquired.

"Not exactly. You are seeing somethin', but it is your imagination only that makes it appear to be a man, one that doesn't speak and appears to be incorporeal, is that not so?"

"Well, yes," Anne conceded.

The gardener bent and retrieved a darkened lantern from the ground at his feet. "The moon is not as bright as it was the night of the ball, but if I hold up this lantern, it will reveal a pattern that looks very much like a ghost." Uncovering the lantern, he stood upon the bench where Theo and Anne had sat and held the light aloft so that the shadows of the branches of the closest tree were caught against the wall of the tomb.

At first Theo was not sure he saw anything unusual, but the longer he stared at it, the more convinced he became that he spotted a face, one with dark, ragged eyes and a round, black mouth. "Look, Anne, do you see it? If you follow the shadow down, you can just make out buttons and even the buckles such as on a pair of old-fashioned shoes."

"I am not so sure I see anything such as you describe, but if you see it Theo, I am persuaded it is there, just as you say."

Baldwin allowed the lantern to fall and jumped to the ground, sending the shadows swinging crazily against the tomb. "As you see, light and shadow play tricks on the mind. I pray that puts an end to your fears of the ghost at Dunsmere."

"Thank you Baldwin. It was good of you to stage this demonstration so deep into the night. As for you, my dear," he said, taking Anne by the hand and leading her away, "you need not fear that anyone of the house of Marcross shall die before their God-appointed time."

"How could we have ever thought a shadow to be a ghost?" she asked with a sigh; she rested her head against his shoulder as they walked, slowly and meanderingly, back to the house. When they reached the steps up to the front portal, he let go her hand and put his arm about her shoulders. "Let us not go in just yet," he murmured as he steered her into the shadows of an ancient oak tree that stood, like its twin, to one side of the grand entrance.

An atmosphere of reticence seemed to fall upon her, but she agreed. As they stepped into the deeper shadows under the tree, there was a shift in the air that had naught to do with the weather. When he dropped his arm from her shoulder to her waist, he felt as if they stood in a country all their own, one devoid of any other inhabitant, human or otherwise.

He knew this was his moment to speak; there had been far too many others he had squandered yet there was one more test of her feelings he felt he must employ before he dared declare himself. Placing an arm to join the other around her waist, he drew her into an embrace.

She did not object as he feared she might and willingly laid her head to rest against his chest. When he felt confident that she had no desire to break away, he put a hand to her chin and tilted her face to rest, skin against skin, along his own. It required that he bend his head, but the feel of her satin-smooth cheek against his was redolent of a heaven of which he had never dared dream.

When he turned his head so that the corner of his mouth brushed against the corner of hers, the unaccustomed contact sent a jolt throughout his body, as breathtaking as it was unexpected. He had delayed marriage until he had found a woman who was as good as she was beautiful; now that he had found her, he was unprepared for the overwhelming hunger he felt for her.

"How long," he murmured, "can I go on like this?"

"Go on…like what?" she asked, her voice alluringly breathless.

"Like this," he moaned, his lungs laboring for breath as, lightly, he drew his lips across her cheek, "wishing to kiss you."

He heard the breath catch in her throat and impatiently endured the tiny pause that prefaced her response. "Have you been? Truly?"

"Yes," he said as he placed a hand behind her head to pull it back while, with the arm that encircled her tiny waist, he drew her to her toes so as to have better access to her lips from his great height. "I have, from the moment I first saw you."

"Oh," she said faintly as he drew her ever closer and searched her eyes for signs that she might oppose his intentions. Finding none, he bent his head and kissed her with a barely restrained passion made up of all his finer feelings of admiration, regard and even worship. When she put her arms around his neck and pulled herself deeper into his kiss, he knew what her answer to his proposal would be.

After a dizzying interlude that left Theo in no doubt as to his future happiness, he emerged from his abstraction long enough to recall that he had not yet asked the crucial question. "Mrs. Crenshaw— my own, dear Anne—will you marry me?"

"Yes, Theo, for I am persuaded I shall love being married to you above all things. But only if you profess always to allow me to be first served from the bacon platter," she said as she stretched upwards for another kiss.

"Dearest girl," Theo said, scarcely able to believe his excellent fortune, "if it suits you, you shall have your own pig!

It was with a great sense of relief that Baldwin watched the Dowager's guests emerge from the trees and enter the house, a sensation that was short lived when the ghost that haunted the house of Crenshaw materialized at his side, his face set in lines of stony anger.

"Why must you tell such falsehoods?" the ghost wailed.

"Surely, you don't expect me to allow you to scare that young woman half out of her wits. And what of Her Grace? She is beside herself with worry as to the possible fate of her grandson."

"But if they do not believe in me, how am I to warn them? It is my fate to warn," moaned the ghost.

"Well then, out with it and be off," Baldwin demanded.

The ghost looked a bit affronted but did not hesitate to speak his piece. "If the current duke does not mend his ways, he shall suffer an ignominious death."

"What ways might those be?"

"His extreme hubris and sense of entitlement, his belief that his good fortune is due to his superiority rather than an accident of birth, his lack of concern for his fellowman, as well as his enormous care for comfort and power at the expense of all whom his life touches."

"What is there in that?" Baldwin asked. "You have described more than half the men and women in the kingdom, titled or not. The Duke is amongst the worst of the lot; I'll give you that. There is not a soul who should mourn his passing nor be in the least surprised that he's dead."

"But I must warn," keened the ghost. "It is my penance."

"Then tell me; what of Sir Anthony? Is he doomed to die in the next year?"

"No, he is safe. Never shall he be doomed to spend eternity warning his descendants of impending disaster."

Baldwin grunted. "Well, that is a relief, to be sure. If that is all, I have my bed to think of."

There came a pause as the ghost seemed to grow in size and transparency. "There is a babe," he intoned.

"There be two babes, one belonging to Sir Anthony and one to the Duke."

"The son of the Duke is my concern. It is with his birth that the line continues, unbroken. So does the evil. He might prove to be the most evil of them all. Take care to keep his feet on the path of righteousness or much of goodness could be lost."

"I will be sure to pass the message along to the Dowager, but I can't promise that she will be eager to share your warning with her son, the Duke."

"He must be warned!" the ghost wailed as it grew ever larger and more translucent so that the clouds scudded through him.

"But what does it have to do with the two of 'em?" Baldwin asked, jabbing his jaw in the direction of Anne and Theo as they lingered at the portal of Dunsmere House.

"Naught, it has naaauuught," wailed the ghost as it loomed so large and thin that it became at one with the night sky of clouds and mist. "They shall be blessed forevermore."

A Rose for Christmas

England, September 1812

Part One

Baldwin, gardener of the Dunsmere estate, deposited the last of the day's accumulation of autumn leaves onto the cerise and titian mound and set it on fire. Although he was more than fond of the vibrant display, it would never do for the oak and Chinese tupelo leaves to obscure the meticulously manicured, emerald green lawn of the Dowager Duchess of Marcross. No, indeed.

Through a haze of smoke, he surveyed the roses that filled the area between the front lawn and the park and saw that all was well. The beautiful rose garden with its dozens of heirloom varieties had originally been planted nearly a century prior and was the pride and joy of the Dowager Duchess of Marcross. If the wind were to pick up and carry the fire in the wrong direction, it was as much as his life was worth. He doubted not that Her Grace would go gladly to the gallows over the loss of her roses; she had very little else she cared to live for save her favorite grandson, Sir Anthony, a man who filled his days with the pursuit of pleasure and precious little else.

However, the arrival of the newly orphaned Ginny six months prior was proving to put a permanent sparkle in the old lady's eyes. The fact that Miss Ginerva Delacourt's first London Season had been just shy of a full-out disaster did not keep the Dowager sunk in poor spirits for long. Indeed, the presence of the young maid, granddaughter of the old lady's beloved brother, had softened many of her ways since Ginny had come to live at Dunsmere.

Preoccupied with his thoughts, he didn't hear the approach of his mistress until she appeared at his side, her face a mask of disapproval.

"Baldwin, I pray you know what you are about, burning these leaves in such proximity to the roses!"

"Yes'm, beggin' your pardon, ma'am," he said with a tug at his cap as he cursed his thoughtlessness. Though he had burned the leaves on the very same patch of ground every autumn since he had been taken on at Dunsmere, he knew the Dowager was particularly fretful this year. She was to enter a new variety of rose at the annual flower show and once she had won, as she was persuaded she must, people would flock from near and far to visit her spectacular rose garden. "I have taken care to cart out a barrel of water in the case it is needed."

The Dowager grunted her approval, and he thought she looked not quite so grim.

"Tomorrow I shall rake the leaves to the verge of the east lawn, if'n it please you, Your Grace."

"As long as it is not too close to the potting shed, mind. Were everything on the property to burn to the ground save the roses and that potting shed I should not care one fig!"

As the potting shed housed the specimen of the Christmas rose they had been developing the past four years, Baldwin cursed himself yet again and bowed deeply to hide the burning of his face. "Yes'm; nothing shall harm any of the roses, I so swear."

He stood upright to see how the Dowager gazed longingly across the lawn in the direction of the potting shed and suppressed a sigh. "If you wait but a moment, Your Grace, I shall have the fire out, and we might see how fares the new rose." He didn't wait for the assent that would surely come but took up the bucket at his feet and dipped it into the barrel on the nearby cart. He put out the fire under her anxious eye, and they walked, side by side, along the circular path from the front of the house to where the potting shed stood at the end of an avenue of ancient limes.

He hadn't even a moment to wonder if the Dowager hadn't yet expelled her store of scoldings before she started in again. "As I am sure you are aware, that foolhardy Squire Barrington cannot be trusted! There are no lengths to which he would not go to foil me. I have born bravely his victories these past few years, knowing I had the beginnings of an absolute triumph propagating in the greenhouse, but what should I find this morning?" she asked in a voice that promised to brook no argument. "The door to the shed was unlocked!"

"Yes, ma'am, it is as you say. I heard the rattle at the door, but as you did not enter, I carried on with my work. I would never leave the Christmas rose unprotected, Your Grace."

The Dowager did not apologize for her misapprehension but only uttered a deep "harrumph", her most common concession to his pride. Nevertheless, her doubt produced an anxiety in him that grew as they drew closer to their objective. He knew he had locked the shed right and tight when he had last closed its door behind him, but he could not help but fret as he fingered the key in his pocket.

As they rounded the curve at the end of the avenue and the potting shed came into view, he saw that all appeared to be in order. It was clear that the door was pulled to and that the padlock hung at the expected angle. When he took it in his hand and gave it a hard tug, it was locked in place, just as expected. Once he had twisted the key in the lock and pushed open the door, however, his soaring spirits plummeted and his knees turned to jelly; the floor of the greenhouse side of the shed was marred with a quantity of broken glass and what remained of the Dowager Duchess' Christmas rose.

Quickly, Baldwin began to calculate the odds that he might be successful in slamming shut the door before the Dowager had a chance to enter, but she pushed past him in a trice. As he watched her face in the pale light of the afternoon, he wanted nothing more than to run, even as he knew it only could serve to delay his punishment. By the time the Dowager's face had turned a deep plum he thought of nothing but the condition of her heart and whether or not he would be needed to catch her before she fell to the glass-and-thorn-littered floor.

Her ensuing screams brought the young mistress running from the house and before long she came through the door of the shed. He could see that she comprehended all with one glance of her lovely gray-green eyes, but she seemed as much at a loss as how to proceed as did he.

"Grandaunt Regina!" the girl called, but the Dowager seemed not to hear. Ginny then turned to Baldwin. "The maids are washing the windows on this side of the house and have heard all. The housekeeper has asked if she should not send for an officer of the law!"

Frantic, he cast about for a chair and managed, with Ginny's help, to get the Dowager seated. As the screams mellowed to low moans, his eyes met those of the girl's over the quivering feather that adorned the Dowager's turban. It was clear that Ginny was terribly shook up and that she depended on him to set matters to rights. If only he knew what was to be done. It was impossible to determine whether the glass was broken by a human or animal, by accident or design. A deer might have torn the rose bush to shreds and dragged its potted roots into the park, yet, it might have been done by a person, as well, someone who had every reason to envy the Dowager her prize rose.

"Baldwin, what can be done? If you haven't a solution, then who?" Ginny beseeched him.

Not for the first time, the pain in her eyes put him in mind of Holly, his own motherless daughter who had no brother or sister with whom to pass the time. She had been but twelve years of age when he and the Dowager had conceived of a rose guaranteed to bloom at Christmas, one with the headiest scent and deepest crimson petals; one that was so perfect in every way, it was sure to win first prize at the annual flower show. How could he return home to tell his Holly that he had failed to protect the Christmas rose they had spoken of so often? It was then Baldwin knew that to return home was exactly what he must do and without delay.

"Take her to the house and set her by the fire with a cup of tea," he instructed Ginny. "I will meet you in the sitting room as soon as may be." Without waiting for a response, he pushed his way out the door at a run, cut his own path through the gracefully curved avenue of lime trees, skirted the mound of autumn leaves and zigzagged his way through the rose beds until he gained the entrance of the cottage he and his daughter shared.

"Holly!" he shouted before he had even opened the door. She was there on the other side, her eyes wide with fear at the tone of his voice. He was in need of catching his breath and was still bent over double, hands on his knees, when he told her what he wanted. "The rose, the one you have been propagating from the Dowager's cast-offs; is it in bloom?"

"Yes, Papa, it is." She went to the window where she had placed a single stem in a vase of water and brought it to him to inspect. It was a rose of exceptional beauty, its petals a bit smaller than the Dowager's version, but with the same deep color and scent.

He stared at the rose, hardly able to believe his good fortune. However, the superior quality of the Dowager's rose was its guaranteed availability of abundant blooms in time for decking the halls. "But, will it yet bloom at Christmas?"

"It bloomed at Christmas last year, Papa, but I can't be sure until it will do so again. The Dowager's rose has bloomed at Christmas for three years running. There is no way of knowing if my poor substitute will ever fare as well prior to the flower show. Surely, it is her rose that shall take the prize."

Baldwin said nothing in reply, only went out the back door to the little walled garden wherein his daughter grew her vegetables and a few roses of her own creation. The Christmas rose was there, awash with blooms that would be full-blown or completely spent within a few days while the flower show was still nearly a week away. Closer inspection revealed a number of new buds that might—or might not—open in time to display their beauty for the show. This was something he would have to worry about later; for now he needed to bring the Dowager hope. He snipped off the loveliest bloom and ran with it back the way he had come.

When he reached the manse, he entered through the front door, ran through the front hall past the astounded butler who dropped his tray in his haste to be out of the gardener's way, and on to the staircase that led to the sitting room. He stopped short when he passed the library and spied the Dowager seated by the fire. Ginny was with her, but the mood was somber in spite of the cheerful flames. The aroma of strong tea rose to meet his nostrils as he burst into the room and two pairs of eyes, full of anticipation, met his. He had always been a man of few words, but there were none that could speak as loudly as did the deep, red bloom he held aloft.

"But, what does it mean, Baldwin?" Ginny implored. "Are we to suppose you have found the very plant, alive and well? That the original was merely displaced?"

"No, Miss, not exactly," he said as he studied the Dowager's reaction. He thought her complexion turned a trifle more ashen at his words. He saw that all her hope was in him and knew that if he failed her, he would be gone. The Dowager was an exacting mistress, but he had never labored for anyone who loved growing things as much as he; the care of her beautiful gardens was his life's work and he must see it through to the end. As such, he must convince her that Holly's rose was a suitable substitute for the Dowager's own.

He bent to kneel at his mistress's feet and placed the rose in her lifeless hand. "Your Grace, this was propagated from the same cuttings we used in the potting shed. It might differ in one minor way or t'other but it is, essentially, the same rose. P'raps you might consider entering it in the contest."

The Dowager's eyes grew large with what he feared to be anger. "By this do you mean to say you have taken cuttings from my prize rose to create this?"

"T'wasn't for myself, Your Grace, but for my daughter; she enjoys puttering about the garden and has no family other than myself as who's always to work. I brought them to her so as to brighten up her days. I can see now that I have done wrong," he said, his head bowed, and his cap twisted into knots in his hands.

"Then, it *is* my rose!" the Dowager demanded, oblivious to his chagrin.

"Not just the same, but close. I believe the petals to be a bit smaller, and there is no way to know if it will bloom at Christmas two years running, though it did the once."

The Dowager sat up a bit straighter and held the bloom to her nose. "I fancy it smells just the same."

Baldwin dared to look up and was gratified to see that the rose had put a bloom in the Dowager's cheeks. "No, not fancy; it smells just as it ought."

"We have done the work, you and I," the Dowager pointed out. "We know my rose performs just as we claim. Who is to know if we entered this plant in its place?"

"You would know, Grandaunt, and I and Baldwin, here," Ginny interjected. "It is *not* your rose. Even if it were precisely the same, it was Holly who grew it."

Baldwin felt his heart squeeze with pain, both for the Dowager and for his daughter who had, indeed, created the rose and whose contribution would never be acknowledged. If the Dowager claimed the rose as her own she would very likely win the competition, but first he would be required to dig it from the earth at his back door and plant it in the heirloom rose garden far from Holly's reach. Torn between love and duty, he stood in anguished silence and waited for his mistress to state her will.

"There is one other," the Dowager said with a moan. "That bothersome Squire Barrington! He will doubtless enter my rose as his own, mark my words if he should not!"

"But Grandaunt, we don't know it was he who took the rose," Ginny insisted. "Besides which, if he had, would he dare to enter it?"

"There is no saying what brazen act that man might commit! I believe he is addled if not downright demented." The Dowager looked a question at Baldwin, one for which he had no answer. "Very well," she announced as she rose to her feet, "I shall take this to my room and retire for the night. I will inform you of my wishes in the morning, Baldwin."

He and Ginny remained silent and frozen in place until the Dowager had taken herself upstairs, whereupon the young maid fell to worrying. "Baldwin, you must see how wrong it would be for Grandaunt to enter that rose," she said as she wrung her hands. "And yet, it is all she has lived for these past few months since we returned from London in such defeat."

Baldwin wished to tell the young maid how much her presence meant to the crotchety, old woman but knew it was not his place. "There is naught to be done, now, but await her pleasure in the morning," he said with a touch of his hand to his cap, whereupon, he took himself off and made his way home, ready to drop into bed as soon as the evening meal was done. However, he realized there was one more task to which he must attend before sleep would come that night; he must tell Holly that her rose must be sacrificed.

As he zigzagged his way through the rose garden, a scene that only an hour hence had been the source of such satisfaction, he felt only anxiety: for himself, for the Dowager, and for his daughter. If Holly chose to keep her rose, would they not become without a home and in need of a job elsewhere? A dismissal from an establishment of such notability as that of the Dowager Duchess would not lend itself to swift re-employment. They would be required to travel far in order to outrun his failure at Dunsmere.

When he entered the cottage, his dinner was laid out for him on the well-scrubbed table in front of a crackling fire designed to chase away the chill of the early autumn night. He waited until they had dined before broaching the subject of the rose and, like the dutiful daughter she was, she asked no questions before he had eaten every last bite and licked his fingers in appreciation. The moment the dishes had been cleared, however, she took up a chair across from him and demanded an explanation.

"There's naught much to tell, lovie, except that something—or someone—has taken off with Her Grace's prize rose."

"Oh, how dreadful!" Holly cried. "Her Grace must be in a taking o'er it, to be sure!"

"That, she is, and there is only one solution to the problem." Baldwin burned with shame even at the thought of saying the words, but say them he must. "You must turn your rose over to the Dowager to enter in the contest."

He saw how his daughter's eyes filled with tears, but her reply was sure and steady. "That be my rose, Papa. It would not be right to enter it as her own."

Baldwin grunted his assent, a salve to her pain he undid with his reply. "You weren't planning to enter your'n, any road. It had no hope of competing against Her Grace's rose; you know that."

"But of course I hadn't planned to enter the competition, Papa. It's only that it wouldn't be my rose any longer, should she take charge of it. But," she added stiffly, "she is the Dowager

Duchess of Marcross, and I am only the gardener's daughter." With that, she finally gave vent to her tears and fled the room for her own chamber.

Baldwin heaved a sigh and wondered if she were best left to herself or if she needed his comfort. If so, it would most likely be of a kind for which he had no gift; the girl needed a mother at a time like this. The sound of her weeping was like a knife in his heart, so he decided it was imperative that he clean up the mess in the potting shed before he retired for bed.

As he left the cottage, his first concern was for the rose garden, as always. It was as it should be, but his visual sweep of the property captured a view of the old, stone chapel nestled in the nearest trees of the park directly off of the carriage drive. Though his duty to the Dowager was clear, that to his daughter was not. Some time on his knees in the chapel seemed a far greater need at the moment. He made his way to the spired edifice, pulled the ring of estate keys from his pocket, and unlocked the door. Morning would be soon enough to attend to the potting shed.

Part Two

The Dowager Duchess of Marcross opened her eyes and measured the faint light of the sun in play with the shadows on the wall and felt it still too early to rise. She had spent a fitful night filled with fractious thoughts of her desecrated rose, the bumptious Squire Barrington and the dilemma that faced her with regard to the rose that even now wafted its perfume towards her from the night table. As weary as she was to the very marrow of her bones, she was far more weary of her bed. She sat up, saw that the fire had not yet been lit, and rang for the maid.

It would be some time before the fire was lit and the room warmed enough for the Dowager to abandon her blankets so, with a sigh, she plumped up her pillows and turned once again to examine the rose grown by the gardener's daughter. It was a fine specimen, every bit as beautiful, as red and headily scented as the Dowager's own. When she thought of how she had been robbed of her opportunity to enter her own rose. . ! The chit who grew this example surely had no intention of entering it herself; the Dowager was entitled, nay, she had a duty to enter Holly's rose in the contest.

Satisfied that the correct decision had been taken, she felt more relaxed than she had all night and fell into a doze, only to be awoken by the maid come to light the fire. The morning was a bit chilly and the antique tester bed far more comfortable than it had been all night, so the Dowager bespoke her breakfast to be brought to her room. Surely, her reticence to breakfast below stairs had nothing to do with the frank and discerning gaze of the prim and proper Ginny Delacourt. Nevertheless, a sound argument for entering the rose under the Dowager's own name must be arrived at, and the sooner the better.

She refused to dress until she felt that her moral underpinnings on the subject were sound, at which time she took more than her usual care and instructed the abigail to arrange her hair as regally as any queen's. High hair gave the petite Dowager a more impressive air, and she suspected she would need every tool of intimidation at her disposal to cow the forthright Ginny. Why the Dowager should let the opinion of such a mite of a girl have naught to say to anything, the Dowager could not fathom; it was a subject best left to itself.

However, on one fact she was fixed; it was best to broach the subject with Baldwin devoid of the presence of others. Though the entire concept had been of the gardener's making, she knew he would feel torn and try as he might, his emotions always showed in his eyes. It was a sight uncomfortable, to be sure, especially when she knew it was her own choices that caused his discomfort. He was only a servant, but she had never before employed a gardener who loved her roses as much as she. No, she mustn't lose him, but, if the matter of the flower show entry could not be settled satisfactorily, she must certainly dismiss him. Even Ginny should be able to see that the Dowager was entering a rose not her own as much for the gardener as for herself.

Confident she had done all that was reasonable in preparation for her day, she descended to the library where she spent most of her hours writing letters, sketching her roses and giving orders. Once she had settled herself and instructed the housekeeper as to the menus for luncheon, tea and dinner, the Dowager rang for the downstairs maid and sent her in search of Baldwin.

He entered the room just as he always did; his head bowed, and his cap squeezed tightly between his hands. "How might I serve you today, Your Grace?"

"I believe there is still a rather large mound of leaves from yesterday to be burned. Doubtless, during the night, more fell and shall need to be dealt with. Do be sure to move them to the east lawn as we discussed yesterday before you put them to the fire."

"Yes'm, it shall be done as you wish. Will there be anything else this morning?"

"Why, yes, come to think of it, there is. I have made a decision with regard to my entry at the flower show," she said with an air of celebration, one at odds with the apprehension she felt at his possible reaction. "I am persuaded your daughter will be honored that I have chosen to enter the rose she propagated from my cast-offs," the Dowager insisted. "Her efforts honor Dunsmere, as well, and its glorious rose garden."

She felt that he took it better than she had expected, though he did shoot her one anxious look from his steadfast, blue eyes before looking down again at his cap.

"Thank you, Your Grace. She is a good girl and will do as she is told. There be one matter of concern, however, if I might be so bold."

"What is it, Baldwin?" Icy fingers of apprehension gripped her heart at his words, but she dared not allow him to know it.

"There is some question as to whether or not the rose will be in bloom in time for the show. Ordinarily I would take it to the greenhouse so as to time the bloom just right, but that is no longer safe. Besides which, the plant is in the ground, and I fear it will go into shock for days after it has been dug up."

"These are difficulties, to be sure, but I am persuaded you shall come up with solutions to all of them," the Dowager said matter-of-factly with just a hint of menace meant to communicate her unwillingness to countenance failure in this endeavor for any reason at all whatsoever.

"Yes'm, I'll see to it. If there is nothing else, I must get to my work."

"Thank you, and Baldwin? You have been with me a long time, have you not." It was a statement rather than a question, one designed to threaten. He nodded his head in acknowledgment, turned and quit the room.

The Dowager, with far more confidence than she felt, picked up the rose she had taken with her from her room and drew in its delicious fragrance. It really was a perfect flower and fated to win the competition. She had done all that was in her power; Baldwin must do the rest.

"Grandaunt Regina, may I enter?" Ginny asked from her place at the door.

"Of course! Do be seated," the Dowager said and indicated a chair across the desk from her own. The girl sat with a steely look in her eyes, one that had often led the Dowager to believe that Ginny, with her unfailing moral code, uncompromising character and unflinching determination, might one day be the perfect bride for the Dowager's grandson, Sir Anthony. He was a good young man, much as his father had been, but he had allowed his heart to be broken and spent his days in aimless idleness. Yes! Ginny would be just the ticket once she had grown into her full beauty.

"Grandaunt, Baldwin has just told me you intend to enter his daughter's rose in the competition. Do you think this wise in light of the Squire?"

The Dowager was startled by the chit's boldness. "You shall show more respect in future, Ginerva! That being said you will be glad to know I spent a sleepless night contemplating this very matter. As such, I have concluded that he should be a fool to enter my rose in the competition. In the end, I cannot credit even the Squire with such stupidity!"

"I don't suppose he shall," Ginny explained, "it is only that, if it were he who took your rose, he will know that the one you have entered is a fraud and might, thereby, expose you."

"What if he shall? He would expose his own perfidy in so doing."

"Perhaps, Grandaunt, but perhaps not. Suppose he did take it. He certainly would not be expecting the rose he stole to be entered! However, when he sees the replacement, he might accuse you before he stops to think how he is pointing the finger of blame at himself, as well."

"Or perhaps he will merely assume I am possessed of more than one plant," the Dowager said in dampening tones. The chit was bright, but it would never do to allow her to believe she was possessed of the superior intellect.

"I pray you are correct, Grandaunt, but there would be no reason for the Squire to take the single bush if there had been others. It would avail him not and would hardly have been worth his efforts."

"I thank you for your opinion, Ginerva," the Dowager replied frostily, "as ill-formed as it may be. Meanwhile, I do believe you are late for your appointment with the dressmaker who should have arrived some moments past."

"Yes, Grandaunt, you are right. I shall be sure to beg her pardon for my tardiness."

"See that you do!" the Dowager called after Ginny's departing figure in a last, woeful attempt at asserting her authority. The possibility that Ginny could very well be correct was one the Dowager refused to entertain for even a moment. However, time would tell.

As the day of the flower show drew near, the Dowager felt increasingly bilious and out of sorts. She found it difficult to look Ginny in the eye and avoided the gardener altogether. She had instructed him to come only when he was sure there should be blooms for the competition and not before. As such, he stayed away. There was a rumor bandied about amongst the servants that he spent a good amount of time in prayer at the chapel. The Dowager thought it very unlikely but she was grateful that he remained unseen, whatever the reason. She could not bear the thought of looking to him with such hope only to be disappointed.

At long last, the day prior to the competition arrived and Baldwin appeared, cap in hand, at the door of the library. She was so startled to see him that she could not speak and was forced merely to nod in acknowledgement of his desire to enter. As he did so, elation filled her heart; his very presence was indicative of success. "Yes, Baldwin, what is it?" she asked, her heart pounding so speedily she barely could find breath to give voice to her words.

"Your Grace, I am very happy to report the rose has bloomed. There is even now one perfect rose and at least two buds that promise to be perfection itself sometime tomorrow."

The Dowager felt an unfamiliar creasing of the skin around her mouth and realized she was smiling in so broad a manner as to be wholly undignified. Yet, she could not bring herself to do otherwise. "At last, all is well! I shall cut the blooms myself at first light. You shall be on hand to take them into your expert care so they will be flush with beauty for the show."

"Yes'm, just as you wish. Perhaps you might tell me where you want me to place the rose once I have dug it up. I have decided it is best to do it directly after you have cut your stems, just before we leave for the town hall."

"I applaud your wisdom, Baldwin. It shall be as you choose," the Dowager said. The blooming of the rose made her feel as if God himself were smiling down on her and she felt at ease for the first time since she had decided to enter the rose of the gardener's daughter in the competition. For the hours that remained prior to the show, she was able to view the face of the gardener with pleasure and even felt able to bear with equanimity what she imagined to be disapproval on the face of her great-niece.

The day of the flower show dawned warm and clear and the buds had opened, just as Baldwin had supposed. He had a vase of water waiting to receive them so the Dowager might bear them in comfort whilst he attended to his next task. So filled with joy was the Dowager that she failed to consider the tears that tracked Holly's cheeks as she watched her father remove the rosebush from its home and take it away.

The hours between the cutting and departing for the show seemed the longest of the Dowager's life but, at last, they were in the carriage and on their way, Ginny at her side and Baldwin up on the box with the driver. Next to the moment when she was pronounced the winner, the Dowager was most looking forward to seeing her grandson, Sir Anthony, as he had promised to come down from town for the show.

"Ginerva, I pray you to be on your best behavior," the Dowager cautioned with her grandson's presence in mind.

"But, of course, Grandaunt, when am I not?" Ginny asked with a confidence the Dowager felt wholly unwarranted.

"A full accounting in answer to your question would be far too disagreeable an endeavor on such a momentous day," she said wryly. "But should I not be satisfied with your manners today, I shall put tending to your reformation at the top of my list for the morrow!"

"Yes, Grandaunt Regina," Ginny said and meekly bowed her head, though she doubtless fumed in silence.

The journey to the county seat where the competition was to be held took far less time than the Dowager had supposed, and she was all aflutter when it came time to disembark and enter the hall at the center of town. She grasped the vase—not the one the gardener had provided but one of antique cranberry glass from her curio cabinet—tightly against her chest as she ascended the outer stairs and went, with Baldwin's aid, through the door. She glanced round the room and spotted the Squire standing behind the section of the table that bore his rose; she was relieved to see it was a paltry yellow of no consequence, and certainly not her Christmas rose.

Whether it was pique or pride that led her to set up her own entry on the table right next him, she could not say. However, the image of the Squire with his eyes bulging in surprise as he beheld her Christmas rose was reason enough. He seemed to recover his aplomb quickly, however, and approached her with a paper in his hands.

"Good afternoon, Your Grace! It is, as always a pleasure, yes, a pleasure to see you! This is the entry form, one that I trust you shall have no trouble filling out, however, in the case you do I am, as ever, at your service."

"Thank you," Her Grace said in a voice cold enough to freeze the Sahara as she daintily took the paper between the tips of her gloved thumb and forefinger. "I am afraid I should have been quite lost without you."

"It is my pleasure, my pleasure, to be sure!" If he were suffering from anxiety over the Dowager's rose, he showed no sign of it.

With a dismissive air, she turned from the Squire and placed her vase on the table. She spent some minutes arranging the blooms to her satisfaction before she addressed Ginny and her demeanor. "Stand up straight, girl, and do wipe that sour expression from your face. We are not burying anyone today!"

"Yes, Ma'am," Ginny said but her air of grief failed to dissipate.

"Do you not recall that my Anthony shall wait on me here, my dear?" she asked more gently and reached up to pinch the girl's cheeks. "There, that is better. You have such a lovely color when you are not white as a ghost."

Her words had the effect she desired as Ginny blushed at her words and her cheeks flooded with pink. "There, that is much better. I am sure you wish to look your best for such a fine gentleman as my Anthony."

At her words, Ginny blushed even more deeply and turned away. Yes, indeed, it was too soon to hope for a match between the two of them but one day all should be arranged as the Dowager wished.

It was Baldwin who returned her attention to the entry form. "I believe you must fill this out, beggin' your pardon," he said and handed her a pencil.

"Oh, my yes, how could I have forgotten?" she asked, her heart as light as a feather and filled with naught but goodwill for all mankind. She need only write her name, (Regina, Dowager Duchess of Marcross) her direction, (Dunsmere) and the name of her entry, (The Christmas Rose) and she had nothing further to do but sign her name; she would leave the details of how the rose was propagated and grown to Baldwin to compose.

However, just as she commenced to write, her eyes filled, inexplicably, with tears. Aghast, she noted that the squire, whom she had all but forgotten until that very moment, seemed to loom unnaturally large at her right. She turned to see how he hovered over her shoulder and beads of perspiration were brought on by his obsequious smile. Suddenly she knew with every fiber of her being that he had the truth. How, she couldn't say, but the realization caused her to see her actions in a new light, and she was ashamed.

She had had no cause to feel shame in many a year. Or, perhaps, she had only been unwilling to allow herself to fall victim to such a lowering emotion. It was far from pleasant, and she looked to her left for assurance from her gardener. Whatever his thoughts, his grave expression, replete with something that might even have been hope, failed to produce the desired support. Ginny, who stood just behind him with her handkerchief to her nose, was looking pointedly away, her disapproval apparent in the rigid lines of her girlish figure.

The Dowager bent to look down once again at the paper she was meant to complete and felt as if she would faint. Quickly, she stood and looked up to see the handsome face of the approaching Anthony, beloved son of her very own John, so good and benevolent, so different from his detestable brother James who dared to live when John had not. She doubted Anthony would have anything to say to the subject of the flower show entry and was reminded that she had established Ginny as a remedy to Anthony's current lack of an acute moral fiber. Yet, she had not cared to weigh Ginny's opinion on the matter of the Christmas rose.

Thoroughly ashamed and determined to do right, she cast about for a means of saving face. If she were to sacrifice first prize at the flower show, she would do so without affording the squire a thimble's-worth of satisfaction. "Baldwin," she crooned as if about to sign her marriage certificate, "how is it your dear daughter spells her name? Am I right to assume it is with a 'y'?"

Though she felt satisfied she witnessed a flash of astonishment in his eyes he responded with a remarkable composure that gave nothing away. "Yes, Your Grace, that is right, H-O-L-L-Y." His self-possession had a most unexpected effect on her poise so that she spelled Baldwin with a 'y', as well, and was so uncharitable as to blame it on the way Ginny had jerked round to stare at her when the Dowager revealed her intentions.

"There we are," she said brightly just as her grandson strode up to the table. "The Holly Rose entered by Holly Baldwin. Yes, that is all as it should be."

"The Holly Rose!" the squire blurted out. "You can't, no indeed, you can't name a rose 'Holly'. It would be, somehow, quite wrong!"

"Holly shall name her rose whatever she pleases," the Dowager said with a haughty air exactly as if she had never been anything but in the right.

"But, Grandmama, I had thought you were vying for the win this year," Sir Anthony said as he leaned over to peck her cheek.

"Yes, I had thought so, too, but someone or some *thing*," she said with a sidelong look at the squire who crouched in the background, "broke into my greenhouse and stole my entry."

"Never say so!" Sir Anthony said with a shake of his head adorned by a strikingly exquisite hat. Taking up his quizzing glass that hung from a gold chain about his neck, he bent to examine the roses. "These are lovely, just the same. Well done, Baldwin!" he said with a smile for the gardener.

"Yes, indeed, they are," the Dowager intoned. "And when all is said and done this day, they shall honor Dunsmere as the winner of the flower show!"

At her words, the squire spun about and stalked off while Baldwin appeared to have something in his eye as he turned hastily away. Ginny laid her hand on the Dowager's arm and gave it a squeeze. "You have done so much good this day, Grandaunt," she said with a tremulous smile.

"Not as much good as you do me, my dear," the Dowager said in spite of herself.

They rode home in excellent spirits as the trophy, a silver rose bowl, reposed in a place of honor on the backwards-facing seat so as to be admired all the way home. It would be collected on the morrow by the committee in order to have it properly engraved, but for now the Dowager was determined to have it within her sight.

Shortly after the carriage had moved through the gates of the estate, it came to a halt and swayed as Baldwin jumped to the ground. He touched his hat and nodded to the ladies and turned to attend to whatever needed doing, or so the Dowager surmised. So suddenly that even she knew not what she was about, she rapped on the quarter light to call him back. He paused and turned, then came forth to open the carriage door.

"Your Grace?" he asked.

The Dowager, still unsure of what it was she intended to say, and afraid whatever it was should prove fatal to her consequence, impulsively took up the trophy and handed it to the gardener. "Here, take this to your Holly and see what she thinks of it. You may bring it back up to the house tomorrow first thing in the morning."

Baldwin stood frozen as if he hadn't comprehended her meaning.

"You must have it," she urged, forcing the bowl into his hands. "It was well-earned."

As if in a daze, Baldwin took the bowl and turned it this way and that so that it sparkled in the last rays of the setting sun. "Ma'am you can't know what this will mean to Holly. I haven't the words."

"No need to thank me, Baldwin. In fact, you may send the girl with the bowl, and we shall discuss the propagating of a new rose for the next time," she said in magnanimous tones.

"Yes'm," he said with the usual meek nod of his head as he shut the door and turned to face his cottage where waited his daughter.

With a sigh, the Dowager folded her hands in her lap and bided her time as she watched the gardener move slowly towards home. The driver rapped on the roof of the carriage in want of a rap in reply that would signal him to drive on, but she took no notice. There was something about the way the gardener squared his shoulders or, more truly, in the way he carried himself that arrested her attention. He had been so happy and should have been most eager to give his daughter the news, yet he seemed to drag his feet.

To her surprise, when he had almost obtained his goal, he sheered off and picked up his pace as he walked in the direction of the stone chapel, the silver bowl winking in his hands as he went.

She knew now that the rumors of his devotion were true, and it brought to mind her own need for gratitude to her Maker. She had won, or as near to it as made no difference, the competition she had so yearned to win, she had a skilled and loyal gardener who would protect her roses and her reputation at any cost, and she had a beloved grandson who held her in affection.

As she rapped on the roof to signal that the driver should carry her to the portals of Dunsmere house, she turned to consider Ginny who sat by her side. She was smiling, but tears tracked her cheeks as she met her grandaunt's gaze with her heart in her eyes.

"Oh, Grandaunt, Baldwin might not have known what to say, but I do not lack for words! This I must tell you: I have often been lonely since my father died. Since coming here, I have felt entirely alone, even in a house filled to the rafters with people. Yet, at this moment, there is no place I should rather be."

As she lowered her head to rest against her grandaunt's shoulder, Regina, the Dowager Duchess of Marcross, realized that this slip of a girl was the greatest gift of all. What was a prize bloom compared to her very own Christmas rose; someone with whom to deck the halls, stir the Figgy pudding and commemorate the day? It was true that Ginny was possessed of a few thorns, but she was someone to love and be loved by in return. In point of fact, if the Dowager played her cards right, Miss Ginny Delacourt should wed the Dowager's dearest grandson and, in time, the sound of children's laughter would fill the rose gardens of Dunsmere once more.

The Lord Who Sneered

England Dec. 10th, 1818

"I assure you, I am not a'tall misunderstood," Julian, Marquis of Trevelin insisted. It was in response to the remark of a visitor from Milan who dared to assume the scar the Marquis bore must consistently lead to the misapprehension of all those around him, for whether he was happy or sad, cheerful or angry, it appeared as if he perpetually sneered. "In point of fact, there is little in life that requires any reply save a sneer," he drawled as he placed his glass on a tray and took himself out onto the veranda to hide his ire.

Or so concluded one Lady Sophie Lundell who observed the entire exchange from her position behind the bats-in-the-belfry Lady Avery and her feathered turban of vast proportions. As it was Lady Sophie's very first ball, she could hardly say whether or not it might reflect poorly upon her should she follow the Marquis into the cool of the night, though she longed to do just that.

It was not that she felt sorry for him. Still, she could hardly do otherwise; the scar at one corner of his mouth did, indeed, create the impression that he continually looked on the world with disdain. It was not the least comfortable when the glance of his ice blue eyes fell on one for he gave the impression he disapproved of everything and everyone.

Still, it was not her compassion she wished to inflict upon him but her insatiable curiosity. Only, how was she to have her inquiries satisfied when they had not been properly introduced? Though she had heard tell of the corrupt Lord Trevelin, had been warned against him by her father in particular, the Marquis hadn't the slightest notion of whom she might be. It seemed impudent in the extreme to follow him out onto the veranda so as to ply him with questions. However, being Lady Sophie Lundell, she did precisely that.

Fully aware that Trevelin had moved to the right after exiting through the full length door, Lady Sophie took care to look straight ahead as she feigned with all of her might that she hadn't the slightest idea he was present. However, once she had gained the stone parapet that divided the veranda from the enormous green lawns, matters came to a standstill. To her chagrin she realized she had counted, perhaps too much, on her beauty to draw him to her side. Of what use, she wondered, were a pair of snow-white shoulders, hair like polished ebony and eyes the color of spring grass if such charms failed to attract? As such, the deep sigh that issued forth from her lungs proved to be nearly sincere.

The second sigh produced a stirring to her right as a man-sized shadow separated from the wall of the house and moved towards her at the parapet.

"Oh!" she gasped, "I had thought myself quite alone."

"Had you?" Trevelin said in so ominous a voice it gave Lady Sophie pause.

"I think I had best go inside," she murmured in an appropriately quavering voice. Privately, she noted that she had become so accomplished a liar that she half believed in her own charade. However, when she turned away, he reached out and grasped her by the forearm to forestall her going.

"What is your name?" he demanded as he looked down his nose at her from eyes hooded, yet perilously alert.

Lady Sophie hadn't the slightest desire to ascertain whether or not he sneered at her, as well, but she could not prevent her gaze from straying to his lips. Even in the dark of the night, it was clear that one end of his mouth was drawn down in a frown, the other drawn up like a perpetually skeptical eyebrow. With nary a thought for the consequences, she wrenched free her arm, took hold of one of the garden lanterns and brought it to his face. It gave her a superior view of the scar that marred his mouth while it illuminated the sweep of rich, dark hair that curled along his forehead and brought fire to the ice-blue eyes. She was tempted to spin on her heel and walk away, but she knew she would acquire no answers without capitulation. "Sir, I am Lady Sophie Lundell," she announced as she placed the lantern on the wall between them. "Perhaps you are acquainted with my father, Viscount Vane?"

Unaccountably, he seemed to relax at her words as he turned his back to the parapet and rested his elbows along it in repose. "Ah! Then I should think you have been properly warned against me."

"To be sure." She lowered her glance so that her eyelashes hid the curiosity certain to be seen in her eyes. "Only, I suspect my father's prejudice towards you to be monstrously unfair."

His air of complacency melted away at this speech, and he turned abruptly away to stare out at the lawn dotted with ancient trees that reached into the sky to form a canopy of branches through which the moonlight fell in fits and starts. "You do," he stated in tones that wavered between doubt and, to her astonishment, hope.

"Yes, indeed. My father is a great embroiderer of the truth. I never believe more than half of all he says."

"I see," he said, yet he seemed to see nothing at all as he continued to stare out beyond the trees. She minded not at all as

it gave her time to peruse his profile, one free of any scar whatsoever and possessed of a strong jaw, a perfect nose, and cheekbones
any woman should envy, against which his dark hair was swept
forward to mingle with his sideburns. In point of fact, he was
most attractive, and she felt the scar to be regrettable. She was
so absorbed with the thought that she barely noticed when he
slipped an object from someplace about his person and held it up
so that it winked in the light of the lantern.

"You had best go inside, Lady Sophie Lundell."

Lady Sophie did not want to go inside. She wanted to find out
what he held in his hand, how he came about that scar and why
he was considered so villainous that her father should warn her to
keep her distance. It was with great deliberation that she moved
nearer and asked, "What is that?"

He glanced at her in some consternation as if he had thought
her already gone. "It's a ring."

"I can see that is so, but why do you look at it with such longing?" She hoped the question might prompt a romantic tale of lost
or, better yet, unrequited love.

He turned to face her, his lids riding low over his eyes and
his sneer as intentional as his words. "Are you certain you wish to
know?"

She perceived he expected her to change her mind, to falter
and flee, but the knowledge merely stiffened her resolve. "Yes, I
do believe so."

He sighed and turned his back to the trees once again so that
she was forced to observe his scar in much closer proximity than
before. "It is a reminder."

"May I ask of what?"

"No, but something tells me you shall, just the same."

She thought she caught the beginnings of a genuine smile
tug at his mouth but could not be certain in light of the scar
that pulled the corner of his mouth, always upwards. The mere

possibility made her smile, herself, at the thought, and she reached to take the ring from him for closer inspection.

"Tell me, of what does it remind you?"

He allowed her to take the ring with an air of surprise that she suspected had less to do with her boldness than his unanticipated surrender. "What else?"

"What? You cannot mean your injury. Surely you never forget it."

"But, of course! I am not accosted by it but once or twice a day in the mirror. The ring, tucked into its place where I am always sure to feel it, reminds me of what others continually see whilst in my presence."

Lady Sophie now had more questions than before. "But, where do you keep it hidden?

"Dear lady, you go too far!"

His indigence seemed to point towards a man with a far finer set of ethics and morals than she was taught to expect from Lord Trevelin. As such, her questions were mounting in number at an alarming pace. Certainly he would not deign to stand on the veranda with her for the entire evening. She must formulate a question that would cut to the heart of the matter.

"Then answer me this," she demanded, her heart racing in anticipation. "Why has my father painted you such a Bluebeard?"

He turned to face her as he leaned into the parapet, one forearm resting along it and the other poised to pluck his ring from her hand. "Surely you have heard tell the story?"

Sophie returned the heavy gold signet ring engraved with a monogram so elaborate as to be indecipherable in the near darkness, and uttered a sigh of exasperation. "Should I inquire if I had?"

"Your kind always do."

"How can you make such an uncongenial remark? We have only just met."

"True, but I am familiar with your sort." He favored her with a look of challenge, then seemed to think better of it as his eyes dropped to the ring he held between his fingers.

"By that you mean that I am young and untried, accustomed to getting my own way and willing to go to great lengths to do so; that I have my father wrapped around my finger like a twine of silk, and attempt to position every man I meet the same."

"Hmmm, yes, that would be the measure of it," he said, then added a hesitant, "perhaps."

"Then I am in some way different?" She suspected she was, though in what manner she did not know.

He drew a deep sigh and turned again to lean over the parapet and face the trees. "It would be best should you return to the party," he said, placing the ring in the palm of his hand and squeezing it tight.

As she was thoroughly enjoying herself, she had no intention of doing any such thing. "Oh? And why is that?" she asked as she turned to rest her arms along the parapet alongside his.

"Because," he said as if addressing one with the wits of a child, "it is not seemly for you to be seen with me."

"Why ever not? You are a peer of the realm, and I am a viscount's daughter. We have both been invited here tonight. We are doing no harm; we are simply conversing."

His head dropped in what seemed to be resignation, and he drew himself up to face her once more. "Then you have *not* heard the tale."

She turned to peer into his face, as well, and looked directly into his eyes so that he might see the truth in hers. "No, I have not."

He gazed back at her for a moment, and she saw how his scrutiny touched her hair, her lips, her throat. Quickly, he placed the ring, large enough to fit over his evening glove, onto a finger of his left hand and clasped the knot of gold in the palm of his right.

"Well then, Lady Sophie, if you wish to know, I shall tell you, but you must look away from me, or I shall not speak."

"Are you afraid I shall think you hideous?" she asked, but he did not answer her that. As she spun about in obedience to his request, she felt her heart squeeze with compassion and determined to refrain from wounding him if she were able. "Then, let us survey the sky, and I shall hear your tale."

"If only it *were* my tale," he mused.

"Whatever do you mean?" she asked as she turned to look at him in curiosity.

"Pray, do not! You must mind your promise or I shall seek out your father. Do not doubt that he shall most certainly send you home."

Lady Sophie could not imagine what harm might arise from studying his face whilst he spoke. Aside from the scar, it was a handsome face in spite of his saturnine expression. There was a hollow look about his eyes as well that stole the light from them. 'T'was a great pity but, perhaps, pity was the very thing of which he wanted no part. "I do promise, my lord."

"Very well, then, if you must have the tale, I shall give it you. It is not a very long one, and when it is over, you might return to the enjoyments of your first ball."

"Why do you presume it to be my first?" She almost turned to him in astonishment but recalled just in time that she must not.

"All unmarried young ladies adorned in silver spangles and eyes of dew are enjoying their first ball."

She had hoped he would say something along the lines of: If you had been out of the schoolroom before now, I should have remembered that face, that hair, those eyes. But he did not. It was all very lowering.

"Then I was wrong to believe I am different." He did not correct her, and she was taken aback at the pain the omission caused her as if hundreds of tiny needles pierced her heart. "Perhaps you are most correct, my lord," she said quietly, "in that I should not be here with you. Mayhap I should find my father and have the whole of it from him; or from Lady Avery or Sir Anthony or anyone else present at the ball tonight."

He grunted his concession. "You might as well have the story from my lips as any other's. I only hoped to prolong the moment when you should walk away from me. I cannot force you to remain if, once I have told you all, you should wish to leave my side. Nevertheless, I pray you shall see fit to keep me company a while longer."

She felt as if she were playing with fire but play with it she must. "Confess all and then shall I decide."

"Very well. As I said, it is not a long tale." He took a deep breath, removed the ring from his finger and placed it on the wall where he might keep it in his sight. "A decade past, I abducted a young girl for the purpose of forcing her to my will. Or so the story goes."

Lady Sophie felt she should, at the very least, gasp. Though she felt his revelation was entirely wicked, she had expected a crime far less predictable and far more romantic. "That is rather dull. Or is there more? Did you hold her at gunpoint? Or perhaps you used a knife?"

"Of course not! I am not so vile a man. And, as it happens, she was not entirely unwilling to run away with me."

"Who was she?"

She felt him shrug against her shoulder. "Nobody knows."

" Surely *you* know, as well as what has happened to her. Did she marry? Or did you bury her out on the heath somewhere?"

He threw back his head and laughed and, forgetting her promise, she turned to catch him with a genuine grin on his face. She was astounded to see that his scar had no power to mar such a smile and that his entire face was transformed from that of the saturnine to the sublime.

"Lady Sophie, you *are* an original. No one has ever before posed such a question," he informed her with a sidelong glance from eyes that still twinkled with merriment.

She could not restrain an answering smile and obediently turned away to stare at the vast lawns before she asked for more. "Then, she is not dead? Of a broken heart? Or a tainted reputation?"

"You make it sound like child's play, but it is not that simple."

"But you promised to tell me the tale," she admonished.

"Yes, I did. I did not, however, promise you the truth." This admission seemed to dislodge a load of care from his shoulders; she could feel the ease of tension from where she stood, and he now seemed nonchalant, almost carefree. She, however, felt like a child who had been fobbed off with a morsel when she might have had the whole cake. Nevertheless, she could see that he was far more amenable at this moment than any other.

"Very well, then. I have made my choice. I shall remain here on the veranda if you shall tell me the whole of it. I shall not forget myself again and look at you as you speak."

"It is no longer of any consequence," he said as he turned once again to rest his side against the parapet. "I can't say why; I don't believe I know the answer. As to any other questions, I am persuaded I must keep my own counsel."

"Then I shall go," she said, her heart falling as she moved towards the lights and the music, but, once again, he was quicker than she and grasped her by the hand. With a great show of reluctance, she allowed him to pull her towards him though her gaze remained downcast.

"I have wronged you, Lady Sophie. I did not lie, but neither did I tell you the truth. I am astounded that you chose to linger as long as you have with such a villain and wish only to part as friends."

She looked up at him and saw not a sneer but a frank and disarming smile and eyes that gazed back at her in full sincerity. "I do not believe, my lord, that you are wicked, in spite of the wickedness you lay claim to. It is my decided impression that you have been assigned much depravity on account of that scar. If you should only smile more often, I suspect others would forget it as completely as have I. Yet, how might one expect such a felicitous circumstance when you insist on never forgetting it, yourself?"

He let go her hand as he took the ring from the parapet and enclosed it in his fist. "I mustn't forget. It would lead to. . .to expectations the realization of which should prove impossible."

She laid a hand on his arm. "I, for one, do not believe anything to be impossible."

He stared down at her white-gloved hand against his black sleeve, then looked up to gaze into her eyes. "If only the world were peopled with Lady Sophies."

His manner extolled greater intimacies, and she did not hesitate to slide her hand down his wrist and grasp his fingers tightly in her own. "Then I am correct in my assumption that the scar came before the loss of your respectability?"

"Is that so extraordinary? He drew his fingers from hers and donned the ring in their place. "Scars such as this hardly appear in one's sleep."

"Yet, if you had no such scar, I am persuaded Society's collective memory of the incident that created it should barely number one year, leave alone ten."

"Touché, Lady Sophie! Any man would envy an intellect such as yours. If the deed that sunk me below reproach were the same as the deed that made the scar, I should concede and gladly, but it was not. In point of fact, my injury was the result of a righteous act if you judge me capable of such. Yet, it led to evil as sure as if the Devil were the author of the whole from the beginning."

"Then the beginning is where you must start."

With a sigh, he turned away from the house to lounge against the stone wall. "It is not a short tale and is one which the hearing of will deprive you of a triumphant splash into society tonight. Yet, if you wish to hear it, I find I cannot say you nay, try as I might."

"Why is that?" she asked as she moved to stand, companionably, by his side.

He favored her with a questioning look from the corner of his eye, one that raked her from head to toe. "It is less than rare when a woman grants me the favor of her presence for longer than it takes to execute a Quadrille, leave alone one of such beauty."

His naked admiration caused Lady Sophie to burn with an emotion with which she had had little acquaintance. It was both exhilarating as well as somewhat distressing and left her casting about for a suitable response. "Handsome is as handsome does, my lord. Those who should shun you for anything as inconsequential as a scar is not worth as much as the time it takes to perform the opening bows."

He had no immediate reply to this. Instead, he lifted his hand so that it hovered over hers for a moment before he snatched it away and uttered a harsh laugh. "And yet I remain more alone than even Bluebeard."

Lady Sophie felt his misery like a cloud of ice over her heart. She thought of her loving father and mother, her bothersome but adoring younger brothers and sister and her devoted governess, all who peopled her life with companionship and affection. How should she find value in a single day of her existence without them? Impulsively, she placed her hand over his fingers so that the ring was thoroughly obscured. "Should it be easier, now, my lord, to tell the story?"

He closed his eyes as if pained beyond measure. "I have no use for your pity, Lady Sophie," he said through gritted teeth. "And I shall tell you naught save my assessment of the weather if you do not remove your hand at once."

Wounded to the core, she did as he commanded. "There is your ring laid bare for your perusal, my lord. I wish you joy of it."

He opened his eyes and looked at the ring as if to sear its image into his mind. "You do not know what game you play at, Lady Sophie."

"I am at no game, my lord. I only wish to see you heart-whole. If that ring holds the origins of your solitude, then why remind yourself continually of what you have suffered?"

He turned his head to stare at her, the expression in his eyes one of misgiving and his mouth pulled taut so that the scar was a white gash in the light of the moon. "The answer to your question is one I cannot abide. Perhaps you might tell me, Lady Sophie, how to choose differently than have I. First, however, you must know whose ring I wear."

She nodded her approval and, with hammering heart, awaited the beginning of what she hoped should prove the rejoinder of her many questions.

"I suppose you have the acquaintance of Mr. Rogers-Reimann, have you not?"

"But of course! He is a close friend of my father. He and his wife have been to visit my home on many occasions."

"Should it surprise you to know that he is my younger cousin?"

"Younger? Yes! But, how odd! I had always thought he was of an age with my Father."

"Indeed," he said with a nod. "It is his habits that have aged him so. However, he was not always such. He was once a young man, more charming than comely, and, though I had always thought him a bit oafish, well-enough admired by the young ladies."

With his words, the intricate design of the ring resolved into a double R. "The ring is his, then, is it not?"

He nodded. "He gave it me in payment for saving his life, or, perhaps, as compensation for my wounds." He ran a finger over

the scar at the corner of his mouth in a gesture Lady Sophie surmised to be a well suppressed inclination.

"But how very admirable!"

"Not as admirable as was his saving mine." He must have seen
her confusion and gave her a wry smile in concession. "He is next
in line to the title," he said with a shrug. "Our national history is
rife with those who have thought nothing of doing violence in
exchange for consequence in the kingdom. Yet, he threw himself
into the thick of the matter rather than leave me to die."

Lady Sophie felt as if much had been left out of the tale. "You
saved his life, he saved yours then gave you the ring, and now you
wear it to remember that you were wounded on his behalf?" She
turned to face him fully, and he did the same, though he kept his
head down in what appeared to be discomfiture.

"Not exactly. You see, my cousin had got himself into trouble.
It involved a woman; there is nothing in that to surprise anyone. He was challenged to a duel, and he asked that I serve as his
second. The irate husband who challenged Evelyn—that is my
cousin," he explained as he looked up to gage her understanding,
"—was ferociously angry. I have never seen anything quite like it.
They dueled with swords, my cousin's choice as he felt he should
have the advantage with his large frame and height. Nevertheless,
righteous anger lent his challenger strength, and a disinclination
to abide by the rules. I knew Evelyn had only moments before he
was cut to ribbons, so I interceded."

"How very brave!" Lady Sophie gasped.

"Not especially. It never occurred to me that my cousin's
challenger should have no care for his actions and would have as
gladly split me in two as Evelyn. My cousin was quick to get the
measure of the man, however, and fended off his assault until the
other second was able to gain control of the challenger. However,
Evelyn was not in time to prevent this," he said with a gesture
indicating the scar.

"Oh, how dreadful!" she exclaimed in suitable awe. "But how could this possibly have led to the evil of which you spoke?"

"It did not, not at first. In fact, the incident induced in me a heretofore unknown fondness for Evelyn. He had saved my life, and I had saved his. There are few bonds stronger that may be forged between two men. After some time passed, however, I realized he was better at falling into scrapes than anyone I had ever known. This took some of the bloom off of the relationship as I was continually required to compensate for his foolishness."

"But, why should you? Certainly one or two incidents should have been enough to induce a decided intolerance for the connection."

"He had saved my life when he might have let me die," the Marquis said, spreading his hands wide. "He could have had my title, my home, my fortune. I believed him to be my friend."

"Yes," she admitted, "I can perceive how you might have felt beholden to him. I believe I might correctly deduce the next pertinent point of the story."

He raised a brow, but overall appeared to be more amused than skeptical.

"But of course it was your cousin who abducted the young woman you spoke of earlier; how could it be otherwise?" she asked, thoroughly convinced the Marquis of Trevelin to be the most noble of men.

He dropped his head and turned the ring round and round on his finger then, quite suddenly, took Lady Sophie's hands in his and looked up to gaze into her eyes. "How could a young girl just out of the schoolroom perceive truths so many others with far more experience have refused to examine for even a single moment?" He searched her face, his pale blue eyes warm and lively and his lips curved upwards in so pleasing a manner that Lady Sophie felt her heart turn over.

"You honor me, my lord, but how did Society, including my own father, fall under the spell of such misapprehension?"

The Marquis sighed as he gently freed her hands from his grasp. "The only way to save the young lady in question was to abduct her myself. She was perfectly safe with me!" he hastened to add with a sharp look for her reaction and did not continue until he was satisfied her good opinion of him was yet intact. "I had all the details of his intentions as I had been privy to so many times before and with which I did nothing. I determined that, this time, I would prevent him from his folly. Demanding that he refrain from his scurrilous ways was pointless; I was convinced he should only laugh at me. So, I arranged for a letter to be delivered to the young lady stating that the hour of the elopement, as she believed it to be, was to be changed to an hour earlier. I had his ring and so was able to make a credible fabrication of his correspondence. Then, all I need do was carry her off before Evelyn arrived on the scene."

Lady Sophie felt the excitement rise in her veins. "How frightened she must have been when she beheld you in the carriage, instead!"

"She was, indeed. It afforded me a splendid opportunity to lecture her on the evils of running off with men, most particularly men such as my cousin, and most effectively, I might add. Once I felt enough time had passed and Evelyn must have given up, I returned her home and released her into the care of her maid."

Lady Sophie was furious. "It must have been she who caused the scandal about you!"

He leaned his elbow along the parapet and relaxed into the stone wall. "How I should have basked in the glow of your anger at the time. But, no, it was not the young lady who spread the news abroad. In point of fact, no one knew of it for some years, save my cousin who effected a very convincing outrage that I had so thwarted his intentions."

"Do you mean to say he was not angry, after all?"

"Yes, but the explanation to that query comes later." He stroked his scar with a long finger before proceeding. "I did believe his anger to be quite genuine at the time and was able to apply the appropriate balm to his outraged sensibilities via a pact: I was to grant him a boon at some point in the future."

"I do perceive how unwise it might have been to make such a promise to one so unscrupulous." Her empathetic nature too strong to be overcome, she once again, laid her hand on his sleeve.

What could be so offensive about such an action, she couldn't say, but he wasted no time in taking her hand from his arm and placing it, very gently, on the parapet after he had first pressed it between both of his. "It was certainly unwise and easily the most imprudent decision of my life. The fruit of my foolishness did not ripen for a number of years, however, when I entered into a betrothal with a lovely young woman, one with whom I was quite madly in love, or so I believed."

Lady Sophie was unable to follow his words carefully, so shaken was she by the sensation of her hand having been held so gently between his own. However, she was brought to full attention when he mentioned the word 'love' in the same sentence as 'betrothed', and hoped they should prove the dawning of a thrilling revelation. "I should presume a belief is the same as the reality, is it not, my lord?" she asked with bated breath.

"No, as it turns out, it is not. However, that was not the tragedy of this particular portion of the story. It was that the young lady believed she loved *me* with all her heart. Pray, do not think me arrogant, Lady Sophie," he said, throwing up a hand. "I was compelled to cry off, and I do believe it should have been easier to bear had she not fancied herself in love."

"But why?" Lady Sophie cried, aghast. Here was the story she had hoped for, one full of lost love, betrayal and tragedy, yet it was no comfort to her now. "I can't believe such a thing of you!" Her own folly at whole-heartedly believing a man she had only just met, one known as the worst sort of rake, was a matter that did not bear examination.

He looked down his nose at her, and she was forcibly reminded of the sneer the scar induced. "You should prefer I defiled an innocent young lady than jilted one at the altar?"

"No, of course not! It's only that, when you spoke of the abduction, I did not know you yet."

He seemed confounded at her confession and studied her visage so unwaveringly she felt she would flinch before he finally spoke. "And you profess to know me, now?"

She pressed her hands together and drew a deep breath. "I believe so but cannot say for certain until I have heard the remainder of your story."

At her words, he turned to the trees, placed his elbow on the parapet and his chin in his hand. "I am sorry to say that my character is only further assassinated from this point on. I think I shall leave the rest of the tale for another time, perhaps when I am old and gray and beyond caring for the warm opinion of angelic young ladies."

Lady Sophie knew she was to blame for his reluctance and cast about for a means to encourage his further revelation. However, his implications as to her nature were so welcome, she found she could think of little else. That he chose to portray her as good rather than beautiful, was as satisfying as it was surprising and she failed to frame a reply for so long she thought he must assume she was contented with the portion of the tale she had thus far heard. When he lowered his arm and turned, she presumed he was intent on returning to the party and threw out her hands to forestall him. Whether he stopped because she wished him to or not, she was never to know, so humiliated was she to find herself with her hands pressed against his chest.

"Oh!" she gasped in reparation but was robbed of further apologies when the thundering of his heart made itself known under her palm. This time, when he collected her hands for removal from his person, he brought them to his lips and kissed the tips of her gloved fingers.

Suddenly she felt rather afraid and pulled her hands from his grasp in the case that the rumors of his depravity were true. Is so, she had fallen under his power exactly like the foolish, untried ingénue she was. "My lord," she said, dismayed by the fact that the availability of air in her lungs was sporadic, at best, "I wonder that neither my father or my mother have sought me as of yet. They are certain to look here momentarily. Perhaps I should return to the dancing."

Lord Trevelin muttered a curse under his breath and paced a few steps away from her. Wrenching the ring from his finger, he once again placed it atop the parapet and braced a hand at each side of it, his arms tense with anger. "Yes, Lady Sophie, you must go, but if you shall, do not think you shall have the remainder of the tale from me at the next ball. Nor shall you have it of another for there is only one besides myself who knows the truth and he is not capable of anything but the vilest of lies."

Lady Sophie knew he referred to Mr. Rogers-Reimann, her father's friend, one whom she had never been given cause to fear. Yet, she could not discount her good opinion of the man who stood on the veranda, staring out past the blackened branches reaching for the sky. She had followed him out into the night to know his story, and she would not be satisfied until she heard the whole of it.

"I do humbly beg your pardon, my lord. I am persuaded Society cares overmuch as to a person's external appearance, and I am saddened that the world should deem you evil because your expression has not always proven to be pleasant. I do not think I should rest if I did not hear how your character became confused with your scar as well as the character of your cousin's."

She thought she saw a relenting of his spirit in the way his arms relaxed, just a trifle, at her words. However, he kept his distance from her as he continued his tale in terse tones.

"My cousin wished to marry my betrothed as she was a great heiress. He demanded that I cry off so that he could comfort her in her sorrow and control her fortune in my stead. When I refused, he reminded me of the boon I had once promised to grant him. Yet, I still refused. To break off an engagement with a young lady is to imply she is not as good as she should be. I could not do that to her; I simply could not." He heaved a great sigh and allowed his arms to drop to his sides. "That was when he threatened to spread foul rumors about her, all untrue but just as damaging as if they were. I reasoned that it would be better should she wed my cousin than to have such things said of her."

"You loved her," Lady Sophie said in a voice that, to her surprise, was laden with sorrow.

"If I had, truly, I should have told him to do his worst and married her, in any event. I should have found the courage to face the rejection of my peers, the ostracization from society, the perpetual banishment into the country. Instead, she became Mrs. Rogers-Reimann, and I am ostracized, just the same."

Lady Sophie could hardly believe the woman she had met any number of times could have once been betrothed to Lord Trevelin, but she felt he did not lie. "What a dreadful story. But how does that assassinate your character? There must be more."

"There is. In order to further poison Mrs. Rogers-Reimann's feelings for me, he put it about that I had ruined the young lady of whom we first spoke. She was finally engaged to be married at the time, but her betrothed cried off when he heard the gossip. No one found any fault in him for so doing, save myself. I went to my cousin in a rage, demanding him to restore her reputation." He turned his back to her and raked a hand through his hair.

It occurred to Lady Sophie that the Marquis was deep in the grip of an emotional pain she could not cure or treat. She wanted to go to him, to take his hand in hers, to murmur words of comfort, but she had not his leave to touch him, not with her hand nor her heart. All she could do was to draw the story from him so that it was fully told.

"And did he do as you asked?"

"No."

She stared at the back of his coat, black as the shadows he faced and considered her next question carefully. "What happened to her?"

"She. . .disappeared." He hung his head as if it were he who had doomed her. "I made inquiries and eventually found her living in London in unspeakable circumstances. I had her moved to a cottage in the country, far away to the north, where she lives out her days."

Lady Sophie felt a new pain clutch her heart. "You call on her there?"

The Marquis spun on his heel to face his accuser. "Never! Not once! I only wished to save her from a life of sin."

Lady Sophie was dizzied by the overwhelming relief that flooded her limbs, and she put a hand to her head. "And your cousin? He does nothing to repent of his sins?"

The Marquis took a step closer and reached out a hand to lay over the ring where it sat atop the parapet. "He felt justified. As he informed me when I demanded reparation, the young lady in question was, indeed, no better than she should be. It was my cousin's doing, the night before I thought to rescue her from his perfidy."

Lady Sophie was so overcome by this betrayal that she felt she might swoon, but Trevelin was at her side, his arm around her waist as he plied the fan she wore looped around her wrist.

"I do not understand, my lord. How could such a thing have happened?"

He gave her a long look and then released her when he had decided she was enough recovered to stand on her own, though his continued concern for her was evident on his face. "It is not my desire to trouble you any further, Lady Sophie. You have given me a great gift that I hesitate to repay with tales of such turpitude."

"But, you mustn't stop now," she implored.

"Very well," he said, favoring her with another long look. "In some manner my cousin surmised I planned to take action to prevent him from fleeing with the young lady. I had thought I was so clever, but he was more so. He never even took out his carriage that night. Instead, with the help of her foolish maid, he found his way to her room the night prior and spent the next in his bed laughing at my naiveté."

"Such treachery!" Lady Sophie gasped. "And Mrs. Rogers-Reimann; she was sacrificed to protect the reputation of such a man! Oh, Lord Trevelin, how you must suffer."

"Yes, but not on her account; our shallow love would not have lasted. I most regret having born the pangs of betrayal at the hand of one I undeservedly trusted, of having been falsely accused, of having been ostracized from society on account of something I was only said to have done. As such, I continually ache for what I have lost; not Mrs. Rogers-Reimann, but someone to love as much as I believed I loved her; for children; for happiness."

She felt the tears start in her eyes and spill down her cheeks. He stood with the scarred side of his mouth in full view yet she did not, could not see it, saw only the sweep of the dark curls against a furrowed brow over downcast eyes. She opened her mouth to say something that might have the power to remove the pain, but none came to her tongue. It was then that the door onto the veranda opened and Lord Trevelin moved so far and so quickly from her side, it was if a gust of wind took him away.

Startled, she looked to see a man coming towards her and thanked the heavens that it was not her father. "Sir Anthony," she said, "how does Lady Crenshaw tonight?"

"She is at home. Our youngest is unwell, and she would not leave him. However, I promised your mother I would attend tonight so as to bespeak a dance with the realm's most recent debutante." It was then that he noticed Lord Trevelin where he stood in the shadows. "Are you in need of any assistance?" he asked as he looked from her to Lord Trevelin and back again.

"Not at all, Sir. Will you convey my best wishes to Lady Crenshaw and your precious boys?"

"Yes, I shall do so with delight," Sir Anthony said congenially even as his eyes narrowed in suspicion. "Lady Sophie, I do believe your mother was asking after you. Will you come with me and make me a keeper of my promises?" He formed his request in the politest of tones but the hand he held out to her brooked no argument.

She knew she dared not refuse unless she wished to suffer the humiliation of having her father fetch her. "Yes, of course, I should love to," she said with convincing enthusiasm as she placed her hand in that of Sir Anthony's and allowed him to lead her inside. However, she was not denied a last glance of the man in the shadows as he returned the ring to its pocket and melted away.

Lady Sophie had not enjoyed her Christmas as much as she ought. The previous fortnight had been replete with holiday parties and balls as well as the much loved traditions that kept her engaged in the creation of kissing balls and shopping for gifts. Yet, she felt none of her usual enthusiasm for any of it. She wondered if it were perhaps that she was no longer a child while she feared it had more to do with the absence of the Marquis from every outing. Even her father had commented on it, claiming Lord Trevelin never missed a party in spite of the fact that he was rarely if ever invited—an intelligence that smote her to the heart.

She puzzled over these things as she waited by the fire in the drawing room prior to the serving of Christmas dinner; in years past she had taken her dinner in the nursery with her younger brothers and sisters yet she felt no excitement at being allowed to celebrate with the adults this year. Fingering the pendant around her neck, a gift from her mother, she wondered why the presents she received this year failed to bring their usual pleasure. They had been selected with the accustomed care and wrapped as gaily as ever, but each time she took one in her hands, the face of the Marquis rose into her mind. In fact, she had thought of him more often than she could rightly recall in the weeks since they had met. She speculated with whom he was marking the holidays and for whom he might choose a gift. Living alone, as he did, would he have bothered to instruct that his home be adorned with mistletoe and holly? Were there any to present him with a gift?

Pining after a man she barely knew seemed foolish, yet she could not help but feel their meeting had been no chance encounter. There was something in the divine in it, a notion that she had become more convinced of as she played for her family the traditional Christmas songs on the pianoforte. The lyrics spoke of hope and love and charity, all of which the Marquis seemed to have lived without for far too long. Tears had started in her eyes at the thought as they did now at the memory and she was startled into the present by a knock at the door followed by the entering of the downstairs maid.

"There be a man below stairs who's insistin' on meetin' with you, my lady," she said with a curtsy.

"Who is it?" Lady Sophie had invited none to dinner, and any her parents had asked should have been shown in immediately.

The maid scurried forth with a small white card and Lady Sophie was astonished to read that it belonged to the Marquis of Trevelin. "Do not show him up; I shall meet him in the library, instead. Tell him I will only be a moment." Lady Sophie then went to the mirror over the mantle and noted that she looked positively alarmed. She wasn't in the least afraid of him, of that she was certain; it was the violent surge of feelings that rose into her breast the moment she learned he waited for her below that had her so afraid.

She took the stairs very slowly so as not to be unbalanced by the hammering of her heart and made her way to the library. To her relief she encountered none who might attempt to prevent her from meeting with the vilified Marquis and, with a deep breath, she pushed open the door.

Lord Trevelin, adorned in buff pantaloons and an azure blue coat that did much to lighten his visage, stood by the fire, his face in profile against the glow of the flames. He turned when he heard her enter, and his eyes widened in disbelief. "Lady Sophie! You have come!"

"But of course. Why should I not?"

"When I was not shown upstairs, I rather expected your father to chase me from the house with a flea in my ear. Isn't a nobleman's library reserved for dealings with unreasonable tradesman and other distasteful interludes?"

Lady Sophie was taken aback. It had not occurred to her that she should shame the Marquis by relegating him to the library or that it would be so revelatory of her desire to keep his presence well disguised from her parents. "I do your beg your pardon, my lord. It is only that our dinner guests are about to descend upon the drawing room. We might go up if you prefer."

"No," he said slowly, his eyes burning with a light she had never before had occasion to witness. "I don't prefer it. It's only that I can hardly credit it."

"Credit what, my lord?" she asked as she took a seat by the fire and indicated that he should sit, as well.

He eyed the chair across from her before he allowed his gaze to return again to her face. "Am I to be so well trusted, then?"

"I have never been given reason to do other than trust you," she said with a dismissive shrug, then remembered her father's admonitions. "That is to say, *you* have never given me reason."

Still, he hesitated to sit until she rose and shut the door so that none should spy the evil Marquis in attendance on the daughter of the house. She swallowed her delight at his wonderment and returned again to her seat. "You must sit, my lord. I trust it has been a Happy Christmas."

With a slight air of incredulity, he sat in the chair she indicated and placed upon his knee a small packet he had been concealing in his hand. It consisted of two tiny boxes, each cheerfully adorned with a red bow. "Thank you. It has been the happiest I have known in many a year," he said with a steady look into her eyes that caused a blush to heat her cheeks. "Happy Christmas to you, also, Lady Sophie. You have been well?"

"Yes, quite well, thank you," she replied just as she ought, though she wondered if a lack of appetite, a loss of interest in all things homely and a decided yearning for the company of a stranger could possibly be considered 'well'. "And you?"

He seemed not to have noticed that she had asked after his health and sat regarding her as if she were cast in bronze or the subject of a painting.

"My lord? I see you have gifts," she pointed out in hopes her words might claim his attention. "How good of you to stop by on your way to dinner with friends, perhaps?"

"Not at all," he replied and looked away. "I have no friends, certainly not amongst those who think me the worst of mankind while I find I have no taste for those who would befriend me in spite of my woeful standing in society. There is only yourself," he

added quietly as he picked up one of the identically sized square
parcels and held it out to her.

"How lovely!" she said, her very soul aching in compassion for
him. "But I have no gift for you. I am persuaded I should not accept
it," she said, pressing the little box into his outstretched hand.

"My dear Lady Sophie, I beg you, open it. If it does not please
you, you may cast it into the fire."

"Oh, no, I am persuaded it should prove inconceivable that
I should dislike any gift from you," she insisted, then feared she
had revealed too much of what was in her heart. "That is, all gifts
should be received with gratitude."

"Then, pray open it," he urged as he favored her with a smile
so broad that the scar she no longer noticed slipped into obscurity.

Silently, she observed that her short acquaintance with this
man had not previously included any scene of benevolence so
long lasting; his appearance was naught but pleasing when he
smiled. As she untied the ribbon, she yearned for the continued
convenience of ensuring he smiled more often than not. However,
she was all bewildered once she had opened the box and saw that
it contained a signet ring with which she was most familiar.

She looked to the Marquis in consternation. "I'm afraid I
don't understand."

"You will." He leaned towards her, took the ring from the
box and held it against the light of the flames in the fireplace. "See
here? The band is inscribed."

She took the ring and peered at the inscription. "*Indignus.*
What does it mean?"

"It is the answer to your question, the reason I kept it always
where I might see or touch it. *Indignus* is a Latin word meaning
unworthy."

Lady Sophie felt herself frown. "But, whom do you deem
unworthy? Mr. Rogers-Reimann? Is this why you cannot forget?
Because you cannot forgive?"

He sat back in his chair, the smile wiped from his face. "No! My dearest Lady Sophie, no. It is only myself, my faults and my folly, of which I need reminding."

"Yet, you told me, that night on the veranda, that the ring was to remind you of impossibilities."

He leaned forward again and took her hand lightly in his own. "Yes, impossible dreams, because I believed myself unworthy of them."

"You? Unworthy?" she demanded. "You have committed no sin, no crime, and rather than use this ring to commemorate how you were wronged, as would so many, you instead operate it as a memorial of your unprofitable shame!"

He seemed undaunted by her outburst. "What then, Lady Sophie, do you think of my gift?"

"That it is no gift at all," she stated and cast the ring into the fire.

He seemed not the least astonished by her actions and together they watched the ring blacken in the flames until finally, he stirred and handed her the identical package. "You are most correct; that was no gift, at least, not one meant for you. Do you recall, when we leaned against the parapet, how I claimed you had given me a great gift?"

"Yes," she admitted and bowed her head. "I confess I did not perceive what it was you meant by it."

He leaned closer and tilted her face to his so that her gaze caught in his own. "None but you has asked to know the truth from my own lips. All assumed they knew, but *you* did not. The evening we spent on the veranda was the first I have spoken those words to a living soul. I have passed the last fortnight imagining my life without the gift you have given me and I confess, I cannot." He took the box from her and pulled off the red ribbon. "Take it, Lady Sophie, take it—and know the gift you have given me."

With trembling fingers, she opened the box. Inside was a simple band, too large for any woman, which bore the image of a golden shield; inscribed thereon was the word *misericordia*. "I regret that I was not taught Latin, my lord," she said as she willed away her disappointment. She had not known until that moment how much she wished to find a ring meant for her own finger. "If I were to guess it's meaning, however, I should be most distressed. It was never my intention to cause you misery."

He threw back his head and laughed, and she knew then that she loved him most desperately.

"But of course!" he exclaimed. "How could I have been so simple? I beg you, dear lady, do not feel reproached for your error; I thought the same when first acquainted with this word. However, I know you shall discover it's true meaning if you but ponder upon it for a moment."

She took the ring and turned it over in her fingers as she tried to learn what he would have her know. Though crestfallen that his gift did not suggest a declaration of love, she was thoroughly intrigued. She thought about the word's possible meaning, but did not feel confident enough to speak until she pondered on how her words and actions might have seemed a gift to the Marquis.

Suddenly, the roots of the Latin word began to take form in her mind; to have accord in misery was to be drawn together in sympathy and compassion. Tears started in her eyes as she dwelt on how she had listened to him, had treated him as a human being rather than an object to be reviled. She had commiserated with him in his sorrow, and she had shown him. . ."Mercy? Is that the true meaning of the word?" she asked as the tears ran freely down her face.

She was astonished when he slid to his knees and took her hands in his. "I shall wear it always, and each time my glance falls upon it, I shall be reminded of how I have been twice blessed. Not only has your mercy freed me of my self-reproach with regard to the past, it has filled me with hope for the future. If one such as yourself is willing to see so far past that which I allowed, perhaps there are others who might do the same. Though, I am persuaded none of them should possibly prove to be so good, so beautiful, nor so courageous as you, Lady Sophie," he murmured, bowing his head over her hands in his own.

Lady Sophie knew she should have been shocked by the sight of his head nearly in her lap but she was not. Nor did she feel ill-used by his trespass of her person. Indeed, she felt she ought to be, but was not in the least, alarmed. Briefly she wondered if she had lost all sense of propriety but how could she doubt when his display of affection felt as welcome and fitting as the breath that filled her lungs? Her gaze fell to the dark locks that curled along his neck and, drawing free one of her hands that trembled without his steadying grasp, she placed it on his head and caressed the waves of brown.

He froze under her hand; too late she recalled his previous distress at her touch and wondered if she hadn't finally offended him past bearing. She had not the opportunity to repent before he lifted his head in astonishment, sending her hand to slip along his brow and downwards, her fingers coming to rest at the corner of his scarred mouth. She felt his muscles stiffen under her caress as if willing himself not to falter, and she wondered how much time had passed since he had last born the weight of any hand to his face but his own. Yet, there was no anger in his eyes as he gazed unwaveringly back at her.

Cautiously, in the case he should object, she ran her fingers across the puckered crease as she had often longed to do and, with a silent sob that convulsed his entire body, he caught her hand in his and pressed it full against his cheek. He closed his eyes, but not in pain or displeasure; there was too much of peace in his expression. When he opened them, the tinge of wariness she hadn't, until that moment, realized was ever-present, had disappeared.

Very slowly, as if she were a bird that might startle and fly away, he drew her hand across his lips to envelop them fully. He watched carefully for her reaction and gently, his eyes welling, kissed the palm of her hand, allowing her to know the full sensation of his damaged mouth upon her flesh. Rather than draw away in revulsion as he seemed to anticipate, she smiled her joy and felt the answering curving of his lips against her skin as tears slipped down his cheeks and over their fingers.

She would have been content to continue as they were forever, and so, when he removed her hand in the same manner as he had the night they had met, her heart sank. She expected him to rise, then, but instead he bent his head and touched his lips to hers. As he moved over her mouth with the same measuring hesitancy as he had her palm, she took care to give no indication that should lead him to believe she could not abide the feel of his scarred lip against her own. In truth, there was naught but the pleasantest of sensations in his touch. When she steadied herself with a hand at the nape of his neck, he renewed his kiss with a startling intensity that left her in no doubt as to his feelings.

When his breathing became ragged, he gave her a final kiss of surpassing tenderness and pulled away. Reclaiming the gold-shielded ring that had dropped to the folds of her skirt, he placed it on his finger, took her hand and drew her up to stand where he could gaze, once again, into her eyes. "Lady Sophie, I scarce dared to hope, much less believe, that you should look on me with any favor. I arrived here today with the longing that you might see fit to stand my friend, with no expectation that you might return my affections. If I lived with naught but your mercy for the rest of my days, it would be enough, my love for you notwithstanding. But now. . ." he said, his face alight with awe, "dare I ask if it is too much to aspire to *your* love, as well? That you might take my name, fill my house with children and banish my solitude?"

Her throat drawn too tight to speak, but happy beyond bearing, Lady Sophie put her hands to his face and gathered it close to anoint his scar with a lingering kiss. His breath caught in his throat as he threw his arms about her and pulled her tight so that the thundering in his chest could be felt against her own. To her delight, he kissed her again but with a passion that had been previously withheld as, locked in his arms, she surrendered to the answering passion that rose within her. They clung to one another so long she was bound to be made late for Christmas dinner but, rather than feel distressed, her heart filled with elation as she realized her touch would never again be rebuffed.

"My darling," he murmured, his eyes bright with a radiance that could have come from nowhere but within, "should I prove ungrateful if I dared hope for more bliss than I enjoy at this moment?"

Lady Sophie gazed at the face she had come to know so well in so short a time, a face that belonged to a changed man, one who had clung for so long to the shadows in his heart and who had finally stepped into the light. "You need not hope," she said, brushing away the last of his tears. "You need only believe."

The End